About the Author

Michaila Oberhoffer was born and raised in the foggy San Francisco Bay area, a place she is still happy to call home. Satisfied with a great meal, a refreshing drink and a bit of nature, Michaila wishes to live life simply doing what she loves. A lover of all things philosophy and science, she believes that being human isn't about being intelligent enough to know but wise enough to question. She can easily be found sitting at a patio table at a coffee shop or at a local brewery, trying very hard to allow the thoughts in her head to become coherent enough to publish, settling for the comforts of humor and speculation. *THE ROOT OF JOHN'S HAPPINESS* is her debut novel.

THE ROOT OF
JOHN'S HAPPINESS

Michaila Oberhoffer

THE ROOT OF
JOHN'S HAPPINESS

Vanguard Press

VANGUARD PAPERBACK

© Copyright **2023**
Michaila Oberhoffer

A CIP catalogue record for this title is
available from the British Library.

ISBN 978 1 80016 711 7

Vanguard Press is an imprint of
Pegasus Elliot Mackenzie Publishers Ltd.
www.pegasuspublishers.com

First Published in **2023**

Vanguard Press
Sheraton House Castle Park
Cambridge England
Printed & Bound in Great Britain

Dedication

To the coffee that drove me, the beer that ailed me, and the loved ones who kept me sane.

I hope to inspire other artists to see their worth and beauty in this world that is so keen on squashing it. I will, however, admit that my cat, Taffy, deserves the main credit as my assistant, but you are all a close second!

Chapter One

John couldn't remember the last time he wasn't happy. He didn't say this to sound conceited; it was just the way his people were since his earliest memory.

Every day like clockwork, he'd wake up and find himself with a smile on his face, going through the motions of his life as if on a permanent loop, blissfully unaware of how empty his rooted happiness was or how futile his purpose was at that point.

One day, on his way to work, he found himself waiting for his train at the local Muni station like he always did, when suddenly a young woman bumped into him. As she pushed past, a paper fell to the ground from her backpack and he instinctively went to hand it back to her, until he realized she had continued her path running in the opposite direction.

Why was she running? he thought. No one ran anywhere anymore; there was no need. And what was she wearing?

He continued to stare in her direction, intrigued by her movement, until he realized he now was becoming the distraction in everyone's path to work. He began to go on his way, thinking how strange this instance was.

He was still holding that single paper in his hand, unaware yet of its significance in his life.

It wasn't until he was sitting on the train in his regular seat, that he realized he was gripping on to that very paper. Like a shock to his senses, he felt that curiosity spark inside him. *I don't remember ever being this curious before.*

He uncrumpled the paper to find a single sentence written plainly in the middle of the otherwise blank piece.

'Why are you so happy?'

Why are you so happy? He laughed to himself as he read such a simple question, thinking how odd of a thing to just carry around. And then it hit him, as he sat there frozen in fear with the predominant smile on his face quickly fading. He found he had no answer. *Why am I so happy?*

All he could muster for an answer was that everyone just *was* happy. Since the dark days of his parents passing over thirty years ago, he felt as if he might have been, in this very moment, the only person in his society who had questioned this. Well, except for that girl. *Who was she? Was she happy?*

During the dark days, his people had found so much stress in their daily life. So much pain and unnecessary sadness blanketed their society, or so he remembered from the propaganda slogans plastered all over their city when he was a kid.

How odd, he had not recalled that memory until now.

It sounds crazy I'm sure, but before this crumpled up piece of paper that could have easily been ignored and discarded at the perfectly accessible waste bin next to every train entrance, John had never found himself questioning his life... questioning this society. It just wasn't something that was done.

Or, at least from his experience, it wasn't something that was discussed. Everyone was simply happy the way they were. It never seemed odd to him, really, because it was their standard of normal. Until this stupid piece of paper ruined his life.

It made him feel like an outsider; made him question everything that he was perfectly happy with moments ago. He felt a strange surge through his body, like a warmth running through him that wasn't welcome, and a narrowing of his sight as he stared blankly at the ground, until he realized what he was doing, with his hands clenched and his face down towards the floor. He lifted his head finding his strange nature had also surprised the people around him, with the many faces of spectators looking at him in confusion, then looking at a poster on the train above his head that he'd never really noticed before.

It read:

'Happiness is a standard. If you are unhappy, we are here to help.'

A number followed the message.

Why had I never noticed this before? He wondered.

Not once in his life, had John remembered feeling this way or had been looked at so questioningly.

I can't be sick.

Why did this frighten him so much? *If I was sick, I could get help,* he thought. That's what they had taught them.

Like a battle in his head, he fought the idea of whether he should tell someone, but fear overpowered him. He sat there and found himself faking a smile in response to their stares, and like clockwork they smiled back and went back to what they had been doing previously. Absolutely nothing. He felt sick; fake; hidden behind this now pretend façade.

He spent the rest of his trip to work with a smile on his face and a busy mind trying to understand, trying to force out this confusion and hoping it would pass, still holding the piece of paper that taunted his reality so.

As he looked around, he kept finding himself wondering if they were all happy too. *Why are they so happy?*

Why is this a bad thing? his subconscious tried to ask him, but it was so strange now after he had been asked why he was happy. He now found that since he did not have an answer to this question, his mind tried to find the most logical step forward. Maybe if he looked at others, or asked them, he might find an answer; the right answer... the *needed* answer.

No, that was too much of a risk.

And then he thought, *What if they aren't happy? I mean, they have to be, right? They're all smiling. I'm not happy, and I'm smiling.*

I'm not happy... He never meant to think such a horrid thought... not happy... This couldn't be true. That would mean he was sick.

You are not sick.

But I must be...

You can't be sick.

It felt as if he was handed a key, and then a door for that key appeared that he never knew was there, and as he went to open the door, the key disappeared from his hand, yet the door remained. Locked, taunting him, begging him to open it.

What was on the other side? Why was he on this side of it? *Which side was free?*

He tried his best to be reasonable, to get himself to stop questioning the purpose of his happiness, because not having an answer only brought him sorrow. But once the question was asked, it became impossible to forget, especially such an intriguing one. And once you begin to look for something, you notice it everywhere. Moments in your everyday life that make you question; that force you to remember the mystery hidden inside *Why am I happy?*

John sighed. *Jeez, I don't remember this commute being so long and so boring.*

Chapter Two

"Are you happy, John?" the woman asked questioningly, but with a confident look on her face that read as if she was trying to appear kind.

It gave a shiver down John's spine when he looked at her too long.

How could she ask such a question and not be corrupted by its purpose? Why did he have such an affliction for it?

When John did not respond, he heard the crisp silence of the room end sharply, as the woman across from him began to write on the bright, white notebook resting on her perfectly crossed legs.

With every flick of her pen on the crisp paper, John felt judgement pierce his barely holding façade, as if it could shatter with a few perfectly placed words from her mouth.

Have you ever noticed that when you try to avoid a question thrown at you so perfectly, hitting your weak spot, that you feel your voice shrivel away and leave you as a weak prey ready for picking; that every moment that passes seems to extend and stretch further than you thought it really must have?

You notice the clicking of the pen so loudly, yet it is feet away from you. The ticking of the clock that seems, even in this slowed-down time, to be moving impossibly slow. The wetting of the woman's lips with her tongue as she prepares herself to speak once again in the silence, your heart beating far out past your realm of comfort.

"You have no need to fear, John. If you are unhappy, then we are here to help."

She said these words as if she truly believed them, but John felt as if her help was a term being used very loosely.

"John, can you hear me?"

The woman spoke once more, looking concerned at John as he realized that he still had not spoken since her initial question presented itself minutes ago.

This probably wasn't going to help him convey his plea of sanity.

"I'm sorry, what was the question?" John asked, forcing a fake smile onto his face, hoping that it was convincing.

The woman smiled back but wrote down more in her notebook, clawing slowly at John's fake shell.

"Is your work satisfying you, John?"

"Very much so."

He was lying. Ever since he cracked the perfect casing over his reality, he felt every aspect of his life begin to shine with the new light of truth. Nothing in his life truly satisfied him.

How long had he been going on like this? How long had any of them? ...

Every day that had passed since that stupid little paper entered his life; John felt that his life was spiraling out of control. He woke up in a bed too small, in a cramped, grey-hued room — grey-hued life, really — to shower in cold water and wear the only thing he had in his closet. It was the same thing he wore every day —his work uniform, which, of course, was also grey.

Even his food was bland. *How could I have been eating this?* he thought with disgust, as he looked in his cupboard for something to coat the blandness of his oatmeal, but he found nothing; just more packets of the same food he had before.

If such a thing even existed.

He tried his best to live his life as he had every day in the past, but everything was different now.

Why did everything have to be different.

With every passing annoyance, dissatisfied bite, itchy jacket and uncomfortable and long train ride to the factory, John became even more convinced that this life must be on the side of the door that was not free. He hoped it wasn't.

If this was free... He wished to not put too much mental effort into this thought — he felt he was depressed enough.

Depressed was another new word in his vocabulary. He found, like puzzle pieces, all of these new feelings and understandings. It filled an emptiness on knowledge in his mind with every growing realization of his tunnel vision. He feared there were more.

Again, not helpful to think about.

Bolt, spring, bolt, nail… One after the other on the assembly line in front of John, like a never-ending spiel of tranquilizer on his mind. With every passing minute he was forced to stand there on the line at work, mindlessly insuring quality of their product at the Jameson Family Production Mil.

Nut, bolt… Oh, look, bolt again. For a second there, I thought I was going to be surprised.

John laughed to himself, causing the workers on either side of him to look at him questioningly. He covered his laughter with a cough, and they all got back to work.

Humor, or rather sarcasm, was a comfort John became fairly familiar with as most people did in times of shaded sun, though he had only just recently found it to be a thing he knew how to do. As if discovering himself, who he was as an individual for the first time. Like learning a language, he found a familiarity and quick understanding on how to implement this newfound nature, as if he had done this his whole life.

He found that he saw himself now as a funny person.

I might be unhappy, but at least I have my humor to keep me warm.

He became so wrapped up in his own understanding of what was around him, that he found himself slipping in and out of his fake happy demeanor from time to time when people would stop and watch him.

Every day on his way to work he looked around, frantically looking for that girl he had run into. It had now been two weeks, but he hadn't found her. He had so many questions and fears he needed to address, and no one was there as an outlet, but to his dismay she was never noticed, nor were his questions blanketed.

He eventually felt himself slipping too far. Yesterday afternoon, he was on the line next to a tall, bald man, about ten years his senior and smiling, like everyone did. He brushed his hands over the lose parts in front of him, sorting them with ease. It was something John was having extreme difficulty doing in the passing weeks, for obvious reasons.

He tried to read the man's name tag, but found he was turned a little far to the right to be read without John putting attention on himself for leaning over to check. All he could make out was the first two letters on his name tag — BI-. He tried to get a better look but then stopped as he remembered that no one did that; in fact, no one moved.

No one talked.

But he had to ask someone.

John cleared his throat and allowed the words to spill out of his mouth before he could stop himself.

"Excuse me…"

The man turned to John with a broad smile. "Oh, I'm sorry, do you need to get through?"

John looked confused, mainly because he was. This man's first response was to assume he was at fault and needed to move to the side. This caught John off guard.

"Um, no, I just… I was wondering. Are you happy at this job? Um… doing this?" John said, ushering to the assembly line in front of them, as the parts began to move past them unchecked and pile up in a very disruptive way.

"Oh, woops. Excuse me," the man said, and began to get back to his work as if nothing had happened.

Well, that did not work very well.

He wished to try again, but he felt the man would only answer the question that he was not ready to have an answer for yet; one he knew, deep down, to be the answer…

He was the only one not happy.

This, however, was answered the next morning when he arrived at his job to find an Employee Satisfaction representative ready to escort him to her office, after reports of irregularity in the workplace, which is where he happened to find himself in this particularly agonizing moment.

"John, I think you might need some help and—"

"No, Ma'am, I'm sorry. I think I just didn't get enough sleep yesterday. I'm fine, really."

She looked at him questioningly, still writing in her notebook, conveying that she thought differently.

"Why don't you take the day off, John — get that rest you need."

John was not sure if this was a trick. He couldn't remember the last time he took a day off.

Had he ever? Did anyone?

"No, really, I'm okay now. Nothing would please me more than to get back to work." He sold it with another smile in her direction.

He was getting too good at this.

"Still, I insist," she said, with a smile back to John, much sharper than his own.

She was the first person he had seen that wasn't inlaid with sincerity. It made him curious, hopeful that he wasn't alone.

Terrified.

"If you insist."

She nodded and ushered him to the door, stating she'd be checking in on him every now and again to ensure he was happy. As he went to leave the room, she ended their conversation with the bone-chilling blanketed phrase he read everywhere, now that he went looking for difference and found repetition plastered everywhere.

"Happiness is a standard, John. If you are unhappy, we are here to help."

Yes, that's kind of what I am afraid of.

He wasn't sure why them offering to help sent alarm bells ringing through his mind, but he felt, for now, at least, it was enough to keep his unhappiness to himself. Until he had some answers, and until he found that girl.

He thought with the day off, he could try to find her. Who knew if he would get this opportunity again?

He packed up his things, grabbed his lunch box, jacket and a quick cup of coffee to go. He wasn't quite sure why he grabbed a cup of coffee to go. He always knew there was coffee at work, but he never felt the need nor desire to grab one. But as if he was now going through the motions of a different mindset, he was craving a cup, and before he realized this irregularity, he was already on his way out the front door.

She can't be too hard to find, right? He thought about how he could realistically go about finding this woman he put so much pressure on to provide the answers he desperately needed.

Logically, she should stick out like a sore thumb in this world. Everyone was the same. Surely, she was not one of them.

That is, if she lives here. I doubt she lives here; how could she? With sadness he realized this was probably true. He had been noticed after a few weeks of subtle nature that was barely considered to be rooting from the same source of difference. *And I was questioned of my happiness.*

He could not stand out more than she did.

The longer John walked and looked around him to find any sign of difference among the tall, grey buildings and the many cement paths leading into unknown directions, he became instituted in his belief that she was probably far gone.

There is only one way to find out... He tried to tell himself.

From his best guess, John could safely estimate that he had, in fact, over fifty different paths jetting off from this spot in front of him, with insurmountable options from those paths leading elsewhere. He unfortunately only knew one. Feeling ill-prepared, and quite frankly, terrified of going down any but the one he knew so well, John found himself instinctively walking down his predetermined path with a new emotion he felt perfectly imbodied his every movement nowadays. This emotion was *anxiety*. It's something we all know too well, a feeling he himself was growing quickly accustomed to, to cover the unknown stress he was presented with in a world now so mysterious and dark.

The grounds floating on the top of his coffee cup that he was so excited to enjoy now became tarnished with his pessimistic world view.

Could I have one moment of joy? he thought angrily.

He stood there waiting for his train, staring at his coffee disapprovingly. He was thankful to find himself finally alone, while everyone, he assumed, was still working.

With relief he allowed himself to let out a sigh, hoping it would carry with it a small fraction of the weight upon his demeanor.

"You know, you're going about this all wrong," a young, crisp voice spoke behind him, startling his presence.

I really should pay better attention to my surroundings.

He turned around to find a girl a few years younger than him — the same girl from before — resting on the half wall which was usually meant to divide the walkway to the fall below between the train tracks. She had one leg perched up and the other crossed under it, resting one arm on her knee casually and the other on the wall. It had never occurred to him to even think of sitting there with so much ample seating provided around him.

Why would I wish to sit there when I have comfy seating right here?

She really is strange.

She sat there swinging her free leg back and forth, just staring at John, looking at him intriguingly. John figured he matched her gaze, both fascinated by each other's differences.

She had loose, curly, red hair, green olive-tinted cloth covering her, with one arm exposed to the elements with what seemed like black marking up and down one of them.

He had short, brown hair that was slicked back, grey slacks and a disheveled, white button-up with a short, grey tie laying on top of it.

They both looked so different from each other that, in that moment, they shared a common thought.

What the hell are you wearing?

"Do you always dress this way? Grey hues, musty suit…" The girl spoke in a judgmental tone.

"I'm sorry?" he replied, defensively.

He honestly never thought to dress differently. More realistically, he did not have anything else to wear, but he felt the insult for it wasn't very subtle.

"I said, you know you are going about this all wrong," she said once more, this time grabbing a bright-red apple from her pocket and taking a bite.

For John, this simple motion of eating an apple was captivating.

What the hell is that? Why is it so bright-red?

John, though his knowledge of the world was limited, did learn in school many years ago about the primary colors that existed, but it was more of a guide, a tool, rather than something to admire. He knew the colors were out there, but he never knew they could be so beautiful, so bright.

The girl noticed his fascination with the simple apple, for she expected such a response.

They always did… such a silly trick. She thought to herself.

"Here." She tossed the apple in John's direction.

Stumbling, he reached for it, dropping his jacket and lunchbox on the ground, as he needed to have whatever it was.

Up close, like a surge in the back of his mind, it hit him. He knew what this was. He had not had one since. Well, that was the thing. He couldn't recall when he last had one, but it must have been a very long time ago.

There was a distant ringing of being handed one by his mother, whose face was hidden and blurred, resting her warm hand on his cheek; him taking a bite of the vibrant apple, his mouth filling with sweet, soft juice.

"H-how could I have forgotten?" he said softly to himself, staring at its simple vibrance, its bright-red beauty. He was so tempted to eat it, but he could not stop staring at it.

"You always do, John. You always do. Let's go."

*

In a location not so far from where John was, in a stuffy office building that from the outside looked like any other building on that block, a woman was walking hurriedly down a blank corridor, walking quick enough to try and prevent herself from being any later than she already was.

The clanking of her expensive heels boomed through the silence with everyone already in the meeting.

Crap, Charlie is not going to be happy.

She reached for the door in front of her, took a deep breath and forced a smile on her face, causing physical pain inside every time she had to do this. She still did not understand why this was necessary; none of them were inflicted. But still she kept her thoughts to herself, as she entered the room which was full of menacing smiles looking in her direction.

Crap, they are mad.

She sat down in her designated chair at the oblong, sleek, white table which was neatly spaced with paper and pens in front of every tall, black, non-swivel chair for every employee in this meeting.

"Right, let me begin," said the woman with short, blonde hair and a perfectly hemmed suit who was holding the only remote for the screen behind her, with everyone's eyes directed to it, ready to pay attention to the weekly presentation.

"So, productivity is at an all-time low with increasing numbers of dissatisfaction amongst the board members. There has been serious consideration to do a city-wide health increase for our citizens. They could be happier, and in turn, more efficient...

"More representatives are being sent out to the production line every day to check the regularity of our workers. Jean, tell me about your recent evaluations." She spoke to the tall, brunette woman to her right.

Why do I always have to go first?

"I only had two evaluations; one today and one yesterday."

The women ushered for her to go on.

"The first one was an employee on the second sector production line that had been complaining about bizarre and disturbing thoughts he had been receiving after a conversation with a fellow employee on the line."

She paused, allowing everyone to take this in. It was exceedingly rare that an evaluation was this severe.

The woman in charge looked concerned. "And what was this conversation?" she asked, both hands on the table, leaning in Jean's direction causing her to clear her throat in a stressful manner.

She chuckled softly, as if trying to imply that she knew her next statement to be silly. "He said that he asked him if he was happy at his job."

The room fell even quieter. The pen spinning in one of the employee's hands seized, and the man across from her sat straight up after having been leaning back comfortably in his chair, though they were built to not be that comfortable.

"Employee satisfaction is not a joke, Jean."

Everyone in the room was now on edge, Jean in particular, looking to their boss, Charlie. She was standing up now, arms crossed, still holding the remote so tight she could break it in exactly four seconds if she wished to apply such pressure.

"Yes, I know Charlie. I never meant to imply it was. It just seemed like such a made-up story… Who would possibly know to ask that? We haven't had an employee dissatisfaction in over ten years."

"Yes, ten years. I say, frankly, we are lucky to have gone this long without one."

This cannot mean what I think it means, can it? They wouldn't...

Silence, being an unwelcome guest to this meeting, appeared once more as if it was an old flame you hadn't ever wished to see again, but happened to show up to the same party you meticulously calculated as the one you'd finally go to, to have that be the one they were invited to as well.

"Is it safe to assume the other evaluation was of the employee in question that had started this conversation?"

"Yes," Jean said, feeling as if she really had stepped in it now.

Just wait until you find out I sent him home, she thought to herself, sweating more than she could visibly hide under this heat lamp of an interrogation.

"And?"

"And he denied it. Said he was happy to work there."

A sigh of relief fell over the employees sitting down, though Charlie was not matching this.

"And you believed him?"

"Well, I had no reason not to. He did seem a little odd. Tired, he said, but not unhappy."

"Jean, please tell me you sent him to his doctor."

She paused, afraid to tell the truth. "No, he said he was tired, so I sent him home."

"What?" Charlie said, with a boom to her voice that cut the sharp stillness in the room like warm butter on toast.

"All right, everybody, this meeting is commenced for now. Joe and Tim, go send out a city-wide initiative. The city-wide annual check-up is being scheduled today. Anyone who misses their appointment will be assumed missing and no longer a citizen of Menos. This is not a drill. Trish and Olive, inform our peace officers of the initiative. Now."

"Jean, you come with me; we have someone we need to talk to."

Jean gulped, frightened by her boss, worried the next words out of her mouth were going to be 'doctor'.

"Who is that?" she said, in a cracked voice.

"The director," Charlie said in a rushed voice, ushering Jean to follow her.

Nope, director is worse than the doctor.

"Charlie, please, why must we go to see the director? We are only supposed to bother him for emergencies. I will find the employee and fix this. You do not need the director to remind me of my job. Please let me fix this."

Her boss waved her hand in the air as a way of hushing Jean from continuing to talk.

"This is bigger than that, Jean. My god, who trained you? Was it Phil? I'm sure it was that idiot."

Ouch. Kicking me while I'm down. Thanks.

"This isn't about you, Jean. I just need you to convey this message to him." Charlie said, as she turned a corner leading straight to an elevator, furiously placing her key card on the electronic pad in front of her until it turned green. She then began to take that wrath out on the elevator up button, until the doors opened up and they both stepped inside.

I have never gone past the tenth floor, Jean thought, as she saw her boss press for level seventy.

"But why?" Jean pressed.

"Because." The woman sighed.

"It's happening again."

"What's happening again?"

"The questions."

Chapter Three

Thirty years Ago

"Tom! Come on, we have to go! They could be here any minute!"

The young woman with long, brown, curly hair flowing freely at her sides, spoke in a rushed manner as she continued to hastily pack away anything she could get her hands on, less concerned with the quality of the object she forcibly stuffed into her duffle and more on the quantity. She was looking for anything and everything to bring with them. Any of this could hold a connection to them; could bring them back should they be inflicted. She tried not to think like that, but it was necessary in times like this. They were only a couple hours away from safety, but the raids were increasing. They could not hide in plain sight — they needed to run.

"Tom!" she said, more concerned having not heard an initial response.

"Yes! Yes, dear, I'm here. I've got John's things packed away. Just getting Lily set! I just need three more minutes!"

"Got it! I'll move to the kitchen!" she said, relieved but in a panic. She threw the duffle over her shoulder, with the paper instructions on how to get to the shelter tucked safely in her mouth. She rushed towards the kitchen, stopping only momentarily to pet their Pitbull, Daisy, on the head and to reassure her that everything was okay. She sat there sweetly, watching her owner throw canned goods and produce into a large, blue bag and then toss a very large bag of dog food on the other shoulder, placing it by the back door. It made her mouth water but she knew she was a good dog, so she sat there, head straight up and butt on the ground, waiting for her owner to call her over to leave.

"All right, Daisy, you ready to go, sweetheart?" the woman said, placing the harness on her softly and securing it. She received a lick to the cheek from Daisy, making her smile in a time she felt lacking joy, and gave her a kiss back. "All right, let's go, girl." She shouted to Tom. "Honey, it's been three minutes!"

"Head to the car; we are on our way now!" Tom shouted back.

She opened the back door that led to their garage, with Daisy following, as she hastily pressed the unlock button on the car keys four times —partly due to shaking, and partly to hurry.

She threw everything in the back and then reorganized it, so that Daisy could jump up in their Bronco onto the red and brown picnic blanket, her favorite toy propped in her mouth, ready to go.

As she went to shout for them once more, she found Tom with Lily in his arms and John holding his hand, with five bags on his shoulders, barely balanced, as he came blundering through the door.

"Here, Penelope, take—"

But she knew what he was implying, and she grabbed Lily out of his arm and carried her over to the other side of the car where she started to buckle her into her car seat. She thought to herself how sweet Lily looked — so innocent and so young. She was only four years old, and she had to leave everything. Penelope shook her head. Maybe it was better that she not remember the world the way it was now. She knew she was being naïve, but she was hopeful that where they were going was guaranteed to be better.

"There you go, my love."

"John, go to Mom. I'll be right there," Tom said to the reluctant seven-year-old holding his hand.

"Come here, sweetie," Penelope said, her arms outstretched, picking John up and giving him a big squeeze as she carried him to the other side of the car.

Tom was forcefully fitting what he could in the back, then gave a soft pet to Daisy and a kiss before he made his way to the driver's seat.

"Who's my brave boy, huh?" Penelope said, as she placed John in his seat next Lily, who was now sucking on her binky, unaware of the mood that was striking John into a scared state, as he was old enough to know something was wrong.

"All right, honey, I'll be right up there, okay?" she said, letting go of John's strong but little hand, which quickly switched to Daisy's collar when his mom went up front. With a comforting lick on the head from Daisy, who was doing her best to comfort John, his mom got in the passenger seat next to his dad, and she reached back to hold his hand.

"There we are honey. All right, we ready?" She now directed her attention to Tom, whose hands hadn't left the steering wheel, looking paler by the second due to squeezing it so tight.

"I don't know about this, Penelope. What if—"

Tom's words were cut off by Penelope giving him a longing kiss.

"I know, my dear, but we have to try. For them."

He nodded, gave his wife one more kiss and then started the car, while pressing the button to the garage door. The stillness of the night sent shivers down his spine. It always did. It was past curfew, and someone would be letting the authorities know soon that they were up.

Penelope straightened out the pieces of paper she had hastily stuck in her back pocket and placed them on her lap, flattening them as best she could.

"Right, here we go," she said, as Tom pulled out of their driveway onto the freshly-laid cement of their quiet cul-de-sac.

*

A couple hours had passed with them on the road, and Tom was finding it hard to keep his eyes open, due to exhaustion and paranoia dictating his driving. He found himself looking in his back mirror more than usual.

"We have to be close dear, right?" he asked, concerned, finally feeling like he was able to not hide his anxiety, with Lily and John having fallen asleep in the back seats about half hour ago.

Penelope was quiet as she hastily looked at the papers under her flashlight, trying to see how far away they were from the next turn. She had grabbed a pen that was tucked behind her ear and placed it in her mouth, knowing she would need it. A moment later, she grabbed the map that was resting under the instructions and marked a road they were approaching, to match the instructions.

"Right, yes, take the next right. We should be there soon — if I read the instructions right, that is."

Tom put on his right blinker, although there was no need. No one should be out this late — it was forbidden. He began changing lanes to get ready to turn.

"I don't like the sound of that. You have to be certain, dear; this is the right way, yes?" Tom said, concerned.

Penelope was always the eccentric one in their relationship, which he loved, but he needed her stability more than ever right now.

"Yes, yes, I'm sure of it. Sorry, I was just trying to lighten the mood. I triple checked it; this is the turn we need to take," Penelope replied, placing a comforting hand on Tom's shoulder, as she looked back lovingly at her kids.

Daisy had made her way to the back seats and was lying with her head placed on John's lap, fast asleep. Normally she would usher her to the back for her safety, but she knew she was just comforting John, and he definitely needed it right now.

"How are they doing?" Tom asked.

"Just fine."

Tom sighed and shook his head before speaking, as he turned right on to the connecting dirt road that Penelope had instructed him to take.

"I can't believe this is happening. How are we going to survive this?"

"We will, Tom."

"But how can you say this — how can you know?" he said, confused and frustrated.

"Because we have to. For them."

"Oh, it's that simple, is it?" Tom said.

"It has to be. Anything more and I can't wrap my head around it. We have to keep going, and we will survive because they need us to."

Tom nodded, though he did not really find her words as comforting as a point-by-point plan. Those were always better in his mind. Blind faith and confidence were never enough for him. He envied Penelope's strength for that.

"Are we sure that it's safe? Where we are going?" he asked.

"It can't be worse than what we are leaving," Penelope said, as she grabbed a bright-red apple from her overall pocket, took a bite and then handed it to Tom to take a bite, too.

"I just hope their generation has the strength to fight this," Tom said softly, taking a bite as well.

"I just hope they still have a reason to," she said, staring at the apple now back in her hand, and then she took another bite with the juice of the apple pouring onto her cheek, as she went to wipe it with the back of her hand.

"God knows that the beauty we hold on to in this world is quickly fading. Let's hope they can learn from our mistakes."

"Or just not make so many of them," Tom said with a soft chuckle, as he brushed Penelope's cheek with the back of his hand.

She reached in to kiss it before he placed it back on the steering wheel.

Another half hour passed, and the dirt road seemed to go on forever, with the sun beginning to reluctantly rise in the distance.

It was a bittersweet experience as the road became more visible, but that made *them* more visible as well. They were unsure whether they wanted to be, just yet.

Trees began to encircle their path the further they went, which they internally thought was comforting, yet intriguing, which in this day in age made them more cautious. If they couldn't see something, they worried what was behind it, though, they thought, in the end it would be good to be on the other side of that for once.

They began to slow down as the road began to narrow and the trees came closer to their car. As the sun crept up, they could see the trees were looking like pine, which was to be expected for their region, though it had been a while since they had seen them so close, making them both smile at the prospect.

Penelope held onto Tom's thigh for comfort as they began to approach a large, wooden gate, with Tom placing both his hands firmly on the steering wheel.

The car came to a complete stop and the silence overcame them, with the only sound being the engine slowly rumbling. They were both too afraid to say anything just yet.

What felt like a minute had passed with them in silence, just staring at the large, wooden gate connected to an even bigger wooden fence, higher than their car. They held each other's hands, just staring forward.

"This must be it," Penelope said softly, breaking the silence. "Kairos..." She read slowly and incorrectly, as if saying it out loud would allow it make sense to her.

She was reading what she could make out of the sign on top of the gate, assuming it was the name of the village they were seeking refuge in.

The gate began to open, and they both looked at each other with an anxious expression that said, 'Ready?'

Tom then put his foot gently on the gas pedal and drove through the now open gate, as it closed behind them.

*

The rose-hued paint lay softly on the otherwise empty canvas as she allowed her mind to empty, and the motions of her well-remembered brush strokes played with her imagination.

Like a calm form of meditation, she moved through the colors on her palate, allowing the flowers in front of her to peek her creativity. She closed her eyes, letting the sun strike her face as she placed the paintbrush in her mouth. She reached to collect her curls in her hands and pulled them into a messy bun, caring more about it being out of her way then how it looked.

John came running up to Penelope, having been playing with the fellow kids in their community, but he had got distracted having passed by his mom painting in one of the many open spaces Kairos had yet to fill. He pulled on his moms' overalls, which were coated in small specks of paint from countless sessions over the years. It was an outfit Penelope didn't seem to want to part with now, for obvious reasons. Penelope smiled at her son, as he ushered to be picked up with another tug of her pant leg.

"Oh, hello, my love, come here," she said with a smile, pulling John up on her lap and giving him a hug. "Pick a color." she said, brushing over his hair that was falling into his line of sight, making a mental note to cut it later tonight, as it grew so fast these days.

She held the paintbrush in her hand and John's, as he pointed to the dark-blue on the palette and they pressed the brush into the paint.

"Great choice, John."

Penelope directed his hand onto the canvas and after a few moments of guiding him, she let go and allowed John to paint as he wished. He moved softer and less purposeful with his actions, but more artistic and free.

It made Penelope smile, as she thought it was exactly what her painting was missing.

Penelope hugged and swayed John on her lap, longing for those moments of perfect comforts, until he got up from her lap to continue to play with the other children in Kairos. He found himself at the perfect age to fit right into the grove of things, something his parents were still struggling with.

Time had passed at their newfound sanctuary, and even with their reservations, they felt themselves getting too comfortable with the safety it provided.

Penelope would find herself waking in a panic almost every morning having felt comfortable enough to sleep through the night, something she hadn't been able to do since before they had John and the epidemic of 'happiness' spread through their world. Penelope always hated that they called it that, saying on many occasions to Tom that 'if they really knew what happiness was, they wouldn't call it that'. To which he would nod in agreement.

But this act of sleeping through the night without fear, without needing to make sure everyone was okay, was going to be a hard habit to break, and when she found herself slipping into this state of peace, it would cause a panic inside. Like internal alarm bells Penelope didn't want this to go away, for she thought to herself, *It's what's kept us alive.*

She tried to remind herself of what her family had gone through, what everyone in Meno went through — the stories she would hear about people waking up 'happy', or rather people being taken in the middle of the night and forced with medication when they realized some people were pretending to take their prescriptions.

It was fortunate that Penelope paid attention to her father all those years. Being one to love the arts, she begged to be released at the dinner table as a kid so she could go paint in peace, but as her father got older and his attention fixated on his work due to illness, Penelope and her brother longed for his scientifical rants that they used to roll their young eyes at before. She still looked back on those late night conversations in her father's lab over a cup of coffee as the reason she was able to go into that field for her family when Meno eventually took over. His words rang through her head every dreadful day in the lab.

'Discovery can easily be manipulated to the desire to control. As long as you understand the theory used to create something, you can find your own solution.'

Penelope always knew her father was a smart man, but his words had never rung truer than when Meno took over. Over the years that Penelope worked at Jameson Mils pharmaceuticals, one of the many manufactures of the medical prescription plants, she paid very close attention to what they were teaching her, and more importantly, what they conveniently left behind glass doors, guarded by a keycard in every one of her supervisor's white coat pockets.

In her father's lab, that at one point was their basement, Penelope and her brother, Liam, found a way to create their own mockup pills that looked and tasted the same to the naked eye. She wished to give herself more credit, but to Penelope it was more of a culinary skill than a scientific achievement. Either way, though, it was huge, because it allowed her and her family to stay hidden without being treated. She felt horrible every day that passed that she didn't mass-produce it, that she didn't just change the supply distributed to all citizens of Meno, but they couldn't risk it, not until they had a way to stop the physicians from treating them.

Otherwise, every citizen would wake up confused, look at the signs plastered everywhere to call their doctor if they felt unwell, go to their doctor and be given the treatment Meno had prescribed to them. Until then, they kept their heads down and did their best to blend in.

It worked for a while — years, in fact — but their band-aid was ripped off furiously when a random inspection took place on their product, and it didn't pass. Panic ensued in Penelope's department, until she saw her brother being taken away by peace officers. Her brother, with a very stern look, told her not to move as she did her best to hide the tears falling down her cheek. She was then informed by her boss that insurances were needed and that she would need to go see her doctor the next day for a checkup. Through hidden pain, Penelope smiled and agreed.

At the end of her shift, she found a letter addressed to her from her brother, with a single line in the center and a map attached to the back of it.

'I'm taking full credit. Save John and Lily. Please don't fight this. I will meet you there. I love you.'

With shaky hands Penelope did what he asked, her palms contorting the once crisp and new paper.

Fighting her pain and agony she feared for her brother and her family, she acted as casually as she could and left the plant at her regular time to not act suspicious. She knew they would be watching her, and she began to mentally plan their escape as she presented a blanketed smile on her face to be intentionally left on the security cameras following her every move.

Her and Tom had spent years planning and meticulously going over how to escape. Now that her brother Liam had found the directions to the mysterious sanctuary, they thought was just a myth, they had no other choice but to trust that her bother had got it from a reliable source.

So they left, with Penelope telling herself her brother would meet them, ignoring her conscience that kept relaying, *He only said that so you would go.*

It had been exactly three months since they had made it to the sanctuary, Kairos. Penelope had learned it was pronounced as in you do not have a *care* in the world, which seemed to be their approach to everything. She received this information from a comical member of the sanctuary, named Hiro. Whether it was true or not they were not sure, but it stuck.

It had been three months and there was still no sign of her brother, something Penelope did not stop obsessing over. It got to the point where she never wanted to get out of bed, but John and Lily needed her, so she forced a smile and got up; a concept that did not go without acknowledgment for what they worked so hard to escape. This, of course, was different, but it was worth her conscience acknowledging all the same.

Tonight, there was going to be another town meeting. They found this to be a periodic event that brought the whole town together, willingly or not.

Everyone was highly encouraged to attend. Most people didn't need it, for in such a small community there wasn't much else going on.

They said it was to discuss any problems people had found in the sanctuary, or any dwindling of resources, but Penelope and Tom quickly realized it was more a place of gossip or simple pleasantries than real actions being implemented or discussed. No matter how good a society seemed, there were always problems, and Kairos could pretend it didn't have any, but to Penelope that was just read more as of naivety of a new society rather than a sign of a good functioning setup.

Part of the problem, as they began to notice early on, was that they didn't like to discuss how the world outside of Kairos was doing. It was like they lived in a bubble outside of the normal society and wished to keep it that way. *Always a good sign for a community — exclusivity from what lead them there.*

"That's how you learn," Tom joked to Penelope in a hushed voice, one particularly slow meeting night, making her softly smile in response.

Every time an 'issue' would arise in the meeting, if you could call it that. Penelope and Tom would give each other weary looks at this, for they much preferred knowing what was going on, rather than become blind to it.

They kept their thoughts to themselves for now, fearing they would be kicked out, but in secret promised to teach their children about the outside world.

"How can they expect things to change if they don't teach their children about what has become of our society? Also, they don't wish to do anything about those still suffering in Meno," Penelope said, baffled.

She was sitting on the porch of their little bungalow, with a pint of beer. Next to her was Tom who was petting Daisy as they watched John and Lily playing in their open garden attaching them to their neighbors. Penelope knew it was a big ask for a small sanctuary in the woods to wish to take on Meno, but her anger and loss drove her annoyance. She was filled with guilt over her brother and was not comfortable with Kairos' ability to forget that world even existed.

Tom took a sip of his beer and continued to pet Daisy softly.

"They are just scared, my love. With time they will grow strength, and with it the importance of knowledge."

Penelope just shook her head, thinking that Tom's years as a professor made him too understanding of people's ways of coping. Penelope, on the other hand, looked at the behavior of her fellow residents as unhealthy, and in a way, selfish. They had spent too much time in this sanctuary that they were happy to just let the outside world, as well as their children's future freedom, perish. Their children were doomed to repeat their mistakes. In her grief, she blamed all of them for her brother being taken, convincing herself that they should have been able to do something, conveniently forgetting the fact that she herself went years doing the same thing in Meno. Penelope wasn't ready to acknowledge any of this and instead found it more of a comfort to complain about Kairos, something Tom was happy to help with, hiding behind his own demons.

"It's just easier to try and forget, to ignore the world outside. Just because a person is scared doesn't mean they should be weak," Penelope said, as one final statement.

Tom didn't respond, feeling he was helping his wife more by allowing her to speak her mind then debate the actions of others. If he was being totally honest with himself, he agreed with her, but he also knew being strong came from having to endure, and they had definitely endured more than most in this sanctuary. But that wasn't to say that he wanted them to suffer as they had.

"We will teach them, Tom. It is important that they know, so they can understand what it genuinely feels like to be happy," Penelope said, with sadness in her voice.

Tom put his arm over her shoulder to comfort her as they watched their children laughing and running around the garden with Daisy, who had gotten up to play with them. That moment of John and Lily running around outside, laughing and free, was something they hadn't been able to see for many, many years; it was exactly what they had dreamed of. It was exactly what her brother had wanted.

Tom smiled. "I think they know, honey."

Penelope smiled softly; it was hard not to, looking at them. "We can only protect them for so long, though. What if this happiness is fleeting?" she asked, as if she was voicing her biggest fear.

"We can't control that, but we can continue to show them what true happiness is; it's the best we can do," Tom said reassuringly to Penelope.

"Since when did you become the hopeful one?" she asked with a laugh, to which Tom reciprocated.

"Well, I can't expect you to always be the chipper one, can I? Besides, I can't help it. This place is growing on me."

"Uh-oh, you're turning into one of them! Quick, say something pessimistic!" Penelope said, with a laugh.

Tom pulled her in to tickle her sides, thinking, in this moment, that they were genuinely happy, and what was even better was that they knew exactly why.

Chapter Four

As John followed the girl, whose bright-red, curly hair flowed freely, he couldn't help but feel comfort in his new 'favorite' emotion; one we are all too familiar with — anxiety. With every step he took outside of his predetermined path that led to only two locations, home and work, he felt his heartbeat quicken and his palms perspire rapidly. It felt wrong or rather strange, like pulling through a thick fog you couldn't see. His arms filled with goosebumps and his breath grew heavy. He surprised himself when he realized that his reaction did not make him fearful, like one would assume. In fact, he seemed to feel... excited. *That's new.*

He watched as she walked casually and confidently down the dirt road that he had never noticed before. He was captivated by the greenery quickly encircling their path. He looked back over his shoulder at the grey train station, wondering how he had never seemed to notice such a change in environment before... the vibrance... the colors... His head hurt from not being used to such stimulation.

Like signals firing in his head, everything he looked at he now recognized, and their terminology became quickly apparent, giving him a headache with every quick recollection.

Tree, bush, lizard, squirrel. He had completely forgotten about *nature*.

How could I have forgotten about something as beautiful as nature?

The young woman he was following had stopped in her tracks and taken a quick right, startling John. He realized early on that she probably wasn't used to people following her, as she jumped down a structure of dark-grey and hard texture.

Rock formation, he thought, quickly realizing what it was.

She didn't seem to care though. She held a confidence of someone who knew who they were, all their quirks and downsides, and simply decided to accept them. As wonderful as this was, John was on the short end of the stick of this trait. She did not seem to be good at guiding someone, and in this moment John could have really used that soft approach.

She then reached for a type of stretchy fabric, put her long curls up in a messy bun, seeming to be more concerned with simply getting the hair out of her face. She began lifting branches off an olive-green, four-wheel vehicle, climbed in the driver's side and sat there with her head out the open door, staring at John questioningly, as he stood their trying to figure out what he was staring at.

"It's a car," she said, scoffing to herself. She pulled her head in, turned the ignition on and gestured for him to get in.

He walked around the other side, clutching the apple with an unnecessary amount of strength, and began to climb into the vehicle. As he put his hand on its outer framing, he was jolted by a memory of driving at high speed in this exact vehicle, shouting in excitement. The wind had been blowing in his face, noises blaring harmoniously, and a blonde woman had been sitting next to him, smiling with her hand out the window, her hair flowing every which way.

"I don't understand," John said confused, coming back to the present moment.

"Blonde, long-haired woman?" she asked in an exhausted kind of way, like they had had this conversation many times before.

John nodded.

She rolled her eyes. "Sure. We went on many road trips together, but no, that's always the memory you have of it. Delilah,." she said, talking to herself, mocking the woman's name as she started the car.

"W-we know each other?" John asked, as he continued to get in the car.

The woman must not have heard him or did not seem to care much for what he was saying, as she placed a tiny metal object with an equally small metal plate hanging off it, into the car. This was all distracting John from the simple task she asked of him; to just get in the car already.

Noise not associated with the engine began to blast through the center console of the car as John got in.

"Before you say it, this is music," she said quickly, seeming to want to get moving.

Music... I love it, though I'm not so sure I like this type in particular.

He finally got himself positioned in his seat that was a lot more fitted than what he was used to on the train. He sat there taking it all in, stunned with overstimulation, as his conscience tried to remind him of just how familiar everything around him was —the melody on the radio, the hum of the engine moving the entirety of the car, and most importantly, the girl sitting in the seat that had a big circular fixture in front of, it with many other gears branching off of it.

She looked at him questioningly, as if waiting for something to appear on his face.

"Anything?" she asked with concern, staring into John's eyes.

Well, at least it seems like she cares about me, John thought to himself, before shaking his head no in response.

She nodded that she understood and then began looking around to check her surroundings before driving off.

Having realized John was simply just sitting there, not really sure what she was expecting, she leaned over him and pulled a cloth strap over his stomach. She then clicked it into a piece of metal, like its sole purpose was to do that.

Meanwhile, in a frustrated tone expecting a million questions she did not seem to feel like answering, she spoke.

"Seatbelt, steering wheel. Pedals —make car go."

John looked at her with a comical look. "Yes, thank you."

Even though he did not know what these things were until she gave him a word to attach to them, he could sense her mocking tone, for it was not subtle, and he felt he could do without it.

She chuckled and then turned a small metal piece attached to a piece of plastic once again into the steering wheel. This time John caught a glimpse of what the piece of metal said that now swung freely. It read *The Final Frontier.* For some reason, this brought up the taste of apple pie in his mouth; warm, crisp apples, buttery crust, caramel filling.

That's a new one, he thought.

As John took a moment, confused and delighted by this realization, the woman backed the car up and then took a right down the dirt road following them.

It was quiet for a little while, except for the music, the car and the young woman's 'rendition' of the music, but to John it all became blurred and slightly silenced, as he fixated on the apple still in his hand, trying to understand what exactly was happening.

"You know, you can eat that apple if you like. Don't worry; there are more where we are going."

"And where are we going exactly?" John asked, confused and begging for answers, although he doubted he would know what to do with them once he got them.

"Kairos," she said simply, as if this was an obvious explanation.

She looked over at him briefly to see that this was not quite sinking in the same as some of the other information.

"Home," she said softly.

"You mean, your home?" John asked, as if correcting her statement with residual fear.

At the same time, he was thinking that he didn't want to handle the idea of everything about his life being a lie.

"Uh, yeah, right," she said, looking over at John.

John did not buy it. He could not believe what was happening, and there seemed to be only one logical explanation to what he was experiencing, no matter how ridiculous or frightening it was.

He sighed and then said, "How many times have I gone through this?"

She hesitated. "Lost track over the years, but this time you guys have been gone for years."

She looked forward and not at him, as if this information was particularly hard for her to say. John didn't respond; he just continued to stare at the apple in his hand, thinking her last words over… *years*.

"You guys? Who else are you referring to?" John asked, but she did not respond.

She seemed to pretend like she was concentrating on the road or that she simply didn't hear him. It felt to John like she was trying to avoid this particular question. John didn't press. Frankly, he was already overwhelmed, and he figured he'd learn eventually. He didn't know anyone besides this woman, and he was still hung up on the fact that this world, in this car full of eclectic forms of stimulation, was apparently his real life.

She must be insane; that's the only explanation. Just go along with it for now. You have no idea how to drive this metal contraption or how to get back, he thought to himself, as a simple way of rationalizing the predicament he found himself in.

Time passed; for how long he was not sure. His attention was fixated no longer on conversation, but with the nature around him; nature he never knew could ever exist. Such vastness, such grandeur, such beauty. He felt so small, and yet, unlike in the city, it brought a sense of comfort. Barren desert led to large rock protrusions with inlays of formation cementing overtime, as if highlighting past formations. Clay-colored rock covered the height of their landscape that spread from a bare, dusty floor. The rocks, as tall as skyscrapers in his city, spread across the entire landscape. He was unsure if it ever ended.

The young woman broke the silence every now and again to bring some clarity to John's perplexed mind. This time it was to inform him that what they were driving through was a 'canyon'.

They continued crawling through the jagged and sporadic terrain that obviously wasn't built to be driven on, though the vehicle they were in didn't seem to mind. In fact, this drive explained why the car seemed to be different colors, depending on what side you were looking at it. Even with the roads' many bumps and turns, she seemed to know exactly where she was going, as she appeared to not pay attention to the path in front of her but fixated the rest of her attention on the music booming through the sound system. She swayed from side to side, vocalizing with its melody. This whole situation made him extremely nervous, as he clutched the bright-red apple in his hand, unsure why he desired to hold on to it so tight.

They were driving for quite some time before they made it to a more established dirt road. All the while he sat there, worried about the fact that it would take him days to get back.

Do you want to go back? his subconscious mind tried to ask him, but he was unsure of his answer.

It was the only life he knew, but something inside him was exhilarated. He wanted to smile. He had discovered a new feeling, and he liked it.

Curiosity.

He found himself smiling, softly and genuinely.

"Ah, see? That didn't take long, did it? I have that effect on people," the woman said with a snarky, sarcastic tone, winking at him in a friendly way.

He chuckled in response. *She's funny, too,* he thought to himself, thankfully.

The terrain then flowed slowly into grassier surroundings, and trees began to replace the empty air. They were passing them so fast that his view became filled with the resemblance of various shades of green brush strokes on a canvas he thought was never possible to be filled.

The smell of the air had never felt so sweet and so thick, and he was surprised when he took a second to recognize the fact that he felt like he could properly breathe again, and it felt familiar. He took a deep breath in, closing his eyes, allowing it to be the only thing on his mind.

He opened his eyes as they took a sharp turn down a more established dirt road, following even more trees.

The curiosity inside him welled up again like a cough he couldn't hold in any longer.

"So, where are we going?" he shouted over the music blasting in the car.

"Huh? Oh right, I already told you. Home, John. We are going home."

"You mean, your home," he corrected her once more.

He hoped she would relay a bit more information besides 'home'. She seemed to be choosing her words very carefully, John thought with a new growing emotion —suspicion. Oddly enough, this did not comfort him like the others did.

She didn't respond, so he just looked at her, searching for the signs of humor to present themselves on her face, but she just looked back at him with the most serious expression he'd seen on her. In his opinion, it did not suit her.

He didn't know what to say or even think. So he stayed silent, but it was hard to think with the music blaring so loudly. He could barely even hear the engine roar.

"Aren't you afraid of getting caught?"

He didn't know why he was afraid of this idea or that it even existed, but something deep inside him was fearful of the people in the city. He was afraid of what they might do to him if they were found to be acting so strangely.

"With every fiber of my being, but what's the point of being awake if you don't enjoy every ounce of life?"

"Awake?" he asked, as if she misspoke. He was offering her a chance to rephrase her statement so it made sense.

"Yes, John, awake."

John felt cheated of understanding, where his own life was concerned, and he felt his voice shrivel away, not wanting to look for answers and find just more questions. The uncertainty, the mystery of his own life, gave him chills.

Why have I never questioned before? Thought to try and remember? I guess that would make things counterproductive for them. Who is them?

His conscience spoke differently — confused, angry. He thought it best to fixate his attention elsewhere than on his own mind in moments like these. He didn't care too much for the copper taste it left on his tongue longing for water. He settled for a dry gulp.

They drove around bends and a passing creek until they finally made it to a more established area, where the trees began to grow in closer until they created a wall, hiding a barely-visible, wood-constructed fence about ten feet high.

"Is this... home?" John asked, terrified, having expected them to be headed to a single house, not an entire town.

"You didn't think I was the only one, did you? I'm not *that* resourceful," she said with a chuckle, as they approached a large, wooden gate.

The word 'Kairos' was imprinted on the gate, weathered and worn over the years, giving John the impression that this community had been here for a long time.

As John read it slowly in his mind, he began to wonder just how many of them were there and whether he should be terrified or excited. *Eh, terrified is more comforting.*

His heart quickened, but the woman driving did not skip a beat as she continued through to the opened doors, and then they were closed behind her by others. It was at this moment that he realized he hadn't even learned this woman's name.

"What's your name?" he asked softly, feeling rude not having asked earlier.

She chuckled as she drove up to a small cottage and turned the car off. "Lily."

As these words rang through his mind, images of his past of being a kid and playing together with a beautiful Pitbull, rushed through his mind. He recalled protecting Lily from a bully that had pulled on her long, then brown curls. He held his jaw, remembering the pain from the punch.

He remembered the road trips, the laughter, the love and the mutual pain in their past that they had bonded over — a pain he still found a fog in his conscience.

She smiled as the look on John's face showed that her name had clicked.

"You do remember," Lily said, giving her brother a long-awaited hug. "I was afraid if I just threw that bombshell on you from the beginning, you might implode. Weakened memories and all that," she said with a laugh, patting her brother's shoulder forcefully, the way only Lily could.

"How... how could I have forgotten?" John asked, with an aching and overwhelmed mind.

"You'd be surprised how often that happens around here; you get used to it," she said, as if brushing this off.

"I don't understand," he said.

He watched her climb out of the Branco and get her supplies out of the back, putting them over her shoulder —an overused backpack, a long, square case and a pair of dirty tennis shoes.

"I know. I'll explain inside, yes? I'm starving," she said, ushering him to join her.

He got out of the car, still clutching the apple. "What are we eating?" he asked excited, thinking of the prospect.

"It will be easier to show you; you won't remember what it is by name. Food requires more sensory recognition, not cognitive."

He looked at her in confusion, a feeling he was really getting sick of, and then began to follow her as she walked into the small bungalow, covered in green foliage, purposefully. He wished for her to explain, but he felt his head was already strained from the constant new stimulation in front of him. So he thought it was best to just take things as they came.

She went to open the door and then paused, giving him another hug that she seemed to have been longing to do for quite some time. "It's been quite some time, brother. I wasn't sure this time whether—" She cut herself off. "Well, anyway, you're back now," she continued, with a forced smile that seemed to normally house a pessimistic expression. "Missed you brother; we all have."

He embraced her back, with blanketed memories of them hugging in the past from the age of four and up, causing a warmth in his heart he did not recognize but wished to never fade away. It was a warmth he hadn't realized, until now, that he'd been lucky enough to feel in his lifetime; that such a feeling even existed.

As they parted and she held the door open for him, he responded curiously, "We?"

By all accounts, one could figure that everyone cramped in this little eclectic bungalow knew each other very well. A warm greeting and bustling for people to greet each other took over the room with a warm glow that overwhelmed John, as people he thought of as strangers came running up and hugging him, and just like a light switch, clarity presented itself to who they were.

A tall, brunette man, about his age, hugged him first.

Parker, one of my oldest friends.

Parker signed, "You all right?"

John instinctively signed back. "Yeah, I guess."

His hands moved before his brain connected what exactly he was doing. Parker smiled at him and gave him a pat on the shoulder.

A tall, young woman with dark, beautiful features and short, black hair, went over and gave him a rough one-armed pat saying, "We missed you, of course. How are you adjusting? It's never easy, this part. Best not to think about it too much, and let the information just emerge."

She smiled, causing John to laugh and smile back, thinking that this probably was some good advice.

Ava, my sister's wife and close confidant, he thought. The one who challenged Lily on who really was the most sarcastic, and yet one of the kindest people he had ever known.

Memories swirled in his head with every introduction and word they spoke. He couldn't believe how easily they came back. Where some connections took like molasses, others just snapped back into place. People seemed to be the easiest so far; that was, of course, once he had a tangible person to attach to first. He even found himself laughing at the jokes they told him, as if he remembered why Parker avoiding Lily's coffee was funny, or simply how well he could understand Parker's sign language and communicate back.

It was weird to think that only half an hour ago, he didn't even know a thing like sign language existed, and here he was, fluent in it; well, so to speak.

John took a moment to look around, and found his senses overwhelmed by eclectic bobbles and trinkets blanketing every bare space. Suddenly a mature, sweet and cheery dog, that looked like a mix of Pittie and Border Collie, came up and licked his hand under the table, making him smile.

"Brandy!" he exclaimed, remembering her clear as day.

His family dog from his childhood days, Daisy, and Ava's dog, Cole, had 'accidently' had puppies, which led to how they met Ava in the first place. Brandy was one of Daisy's and Cole's puppies.

Ava came back in the room carrying their black cat, Achilles, who was resting comfortably on her shoulder. He was trying to reach one hanging bobbles, just out of reach, next to the potted plants and softly stacked books on the built-in bookshelf hugging the entrance way.

"Oy! Brandy, don't be begging for food already," Ava said with a laugh, petting Achilles in her arms.

Lily began putting plates out on the cluttered table, that once was filled with craft activities that Ava and Parker started collecting to put on the side table behind them.

John sat there smiling, petting Brandy as memories of Daisy, Cole and Brandy swirled in his head, causing a soft tear to fall down his cheek as he remembered her passing.

"Yeah, that honestly is the worst part of losing your memories, in my opinion having to re-remember those we lost. She was the best dog," Lily said, putting another harsh pat on Johns shoulder that one would assume was intended to be comforting.

John softly smiled at Brandy who was none the wiser, just licking his face.

"I agree. I miss Cole every day, and of course, my mum," Ava said, petting Achilles in her arms.

"Yeah, my father, too. That and not knowing how to sign," Parker said with a laugh, making everyone softly chuckle at his dark humor, but all had looks of pain, recalling all of their hardships they normally tucked very far away.

"All right, everyone, tuck in; food's ready," Lily said, placing a big pot on the middle of the table under a floral potholder, and handed a bowl to everyone.

As everyone began to eagerly grab some food and fight over the ladle, John was still hung up on their conversation.

"Wait a second. Are you to tell me you guys have also gone through *this*?" John said with surprise, talking about his memory loss, or whatever it was he was experiencing.

They all looked at him with a soft laugh.

"Of course we have; we all have," Ava said, with Lily and Parker nodding in agreement.

"I don't think Meno likes us very much. We defy their limitations," Lily said with a wink and a smile, making everyone laugh.

Meno's name grew a burning hatred inside, recalling a fogged-over memory of them that John didn't understand. He just had a strong inkling they had had a personal connection to his life and that of his family's. He couldn't remember why he hated them so much, just that he did.

His fist tightened on the metal he was holding. *Spoon, right.*

Lily put a hand on John's shoulder, a little softer this time. "I know."

"Who Is Meno? And why do I hate them so much?" John asked, hating to ask others to explain his own emotions, though no one seemed to acknowledge this uncomfortable pattern. In fact, it seemed to fit right in with their conversations.

"They run the city. They are the ones who took your questioning; your ability to think —what made you, *you.*" Parker signed, seeming to have a tough time explaining this.

By the look on Lilly and Ava's faces, they seemed to have no better way of saying it, either.

John didn't say anything. He hoped his words would bring everything back, but the harder he pressed to search for answers, the more it hurt his head.

"It will take time to come back. Just eat; it helps," Ava tried to reassure John as he sat there, his eyes closed and fists clenched.

Lily handed him a bowl as he opened his eyes. He didn't feel too much like eating with everything going on, but the smell and the look of the amazing dish in front of him made him quickly change his mind. After all, this did seem much more exciting than the apple, which he hadn't thought was possible.

"Eat up, John, this is the best part in my opinion — food," Parker signed, and they all nodded in agreement.

The waft alone was intoxicating. He never thought sustenance could ever smell so good. His mouth filled with saliva, as he began to associate the scent.

Garlic, butter, rosemary, thyme, chicken, wine, carrots, celery; happy memories of his mom making this exact dish, teaching him and his sister how to make it themselves; his mom hugging his dad, as they swayed to swing music while stirring the big pot; him feeding Daisy, when he was a young kid, and then laughing as she proceeded to lick his face as a big thank you; being sick and lying in bed and his father feeding him before they both fell asleep together, after reading one of his dad's favorite books. It was enough comfort to make him want to lie down, but he first needed to taste.

"Chicken stew — one of Mom's specialties," Lily said, handing John a full bowl.

He didn't think it was possible, but the smell didn't even do the dish justice. It was as if different colors were swirling together and bursting into beautiful collections of bright silhouettes of sensation. Senses he never knew he had were all stimulated, and he wondered, in that moment, if anything could be as amazing as the beauty of food.

He forgot real quick, the anger he was feeling moments ago.

"See, it helps," Ava said, with a soft smile to John and a wink to Lily. "Always delicious, my love — Penelope would be proud."

Lily's cheeks went red as she reached over in admiration.

Like with any good dish, the conversation had stopped momentarily as no one seemed to be able to part from their food for a moment to talk. The first portion came and went, and they were all on to their second serving.

"Better than the apple?" Lily joked. to which John nodded in reply with a laugh back.

"So, where's Mom and Dad?" he asked, thinking of them as he ate the dish that was so connected to his childhood, finding comfort in the fact that he didn't remember them passing, though he feared he just hadn't fully remembered that.

"They are both alive," Lily assured, knowing that was a fear they both shared in this state. "So, get that idea out of your head." She then looked at Ava and Parker and sighed. "They are both in the city."

Parker and Ava just looked down at their bowls as if something particularly interesting rested in it, and John looked confused and anxious by his sister's words.

"I'm getting from your tone that that *isn't* a good thing?" John asked, confused.

They all were now looking at Lily, making her uncomfortable, so she got up abruptly and started rummaging through a lower cupboard in the kitchen, stopping momentarily to pull the curious Achilles out of that very cupboard. She then pulled out a dark-green, tall bottle containing an even darker liquid.

"I've got a lot of explaining to do. Your mind never likes remembering this part — mine either," Lily said, sitting back down and pulling the already-pulled cork out of the half-empty bottle. "This is wine; you're going to like it."

She began pouring the velvety, ruby-red liquid into all of their empty glasses. A fruity, cinnamon, almost warming, sharp scent wafted through the room.

John sat on the edge of his seat while his sister began to explain their complicated past. Ava and Parker sat as uneasy spectators, taking a few rather large sips from their glasses. They seemed to really like wine, or for some unknown reason to John, needed it.

Chapter Five

Approximately Twenty-Nine years ago

Penelope wondered whether she would ever find normalcy or whether she would ever want that. She never was the type of person who wanted anything normal to happen in her life, and in most cases this would be entirely correct, but living in the city changed a person. It had changed her. So much about their life in the city was out of their control, and though she loved her quirks and differences even more, one could even suggest that that's why she pursued the arts so strongly. It was a way of expression like no other, but that was just what interested Penelope.

Everything else, though, was built out of a desire to not only be anything and express herself uniquely, but to finally be able to do it publicly. That was the true dream for most in the city, and Penelope was no different. When you had to hide away and pretend to not have human desires or uniqueness — which was seen as such a sickness — you'd be surprised how quickly you wished for normalcy, that others attached so nonchalantly to. The normalcy of sitting at a small, black, metal table and chairs outside your local coffee shop; sipping those life-giving cups of coffee and soaking in that oh-so-sweet sun; smiling casually with not a care in the world of what others thought about your mohawk and leather jacket in the middle of summer. To be clear, as this was pertinent to her character, she did not wish to be *normal*. She wished that who she was naturally and who people genuinely were, *was* what was normal; not caring because you were able to…. That was what Penelope wanted for her family, and more specifically, for herself.

And yet, she had that. Kairos was that salvation she had longed for, for so long. But then, why was she still on edge? Why did she fear for her safety and that of her family? They were finally safe.

She was not convinced. That was probably because there was no grand difference here in Kairos besides the lush, and some would even say, 'harsh' environment. The lack of forced smiling was life-changing, but that was it. She still got looks of judgement, and the fear of influence was still lingering in the air, though no one seemed to press such standards. Penelope wondered if it was left over from Meno's rule and if it was all in her head, but if she listened to her instincts, she would notice it wasn't just in her head.

"It's what people are comfortable in. Did you expect a big neon boa on every citizen?" Tom said comically, making Penelope laugh, as they enjoyed a pint in their back garden, having put John and Lily to bed a little while ago.

"Of course not, but something — anything — to signify that people were—" Penelope sighed, unsure of how to say what she wanted to without sounding rude.

"That they are different? Genuinely happy to be here?" Tom pressed.

"I guess. I don't know. I sound like the director; wanting people to smile and be happy. That's not my intention at all."

"Darling, I know. It's not what I expected, either. Everyone is so—"

"Quiet," Penelope interjected, finishing his statement for him.

"Yeah, it's weird. But to be fair, we don't know what normal is, do we? And this whole community is built off the idea of not having to be, you know? Their expression could simply just be boring, and that's okay," Tom replied.

"Is it though?" Penelope said in a joking manner.

Tom laughed.

"I know, you're right," Penelope continued. "I'm just... I can't believe I'm about to complain about this. I'm bored, Tom, truly bored." She laughed softly.

Tom laughed as well. "I know; I am too."

"Never satisfied, are we?" Penelope said with a chuckle.

"Never," Tom responded with a smile, as he pulled Penelope in for a one-armed hug, and she gratefully nestled into his chest.

"Well, at least we now have more time for this." Tom replied, brushing a curl out of Penelope's face and kissing her deeply, causing her to chuckle as he kept going, forcing them to now be laying down on the porch, beers discarded on the side.

"I guess this isn't too bad, is it?" Penelope replied, kissing Tom back.

Then why am I terrified? she thought, keeping these contemplations to herself, not wanting to ruin the moment with her overthinking and it was in fact, a great moment.

*

"Honey, look at me," A lady with long, braided, blonde hair said with a sigh, as she tried very frustratingly to capture the attention of her young son, who was more distracted with the pink hibiscus blooming around the council meeting headquarters.

The weekly meeting had just ended, and everyone was lulled, ready for sleep, with nothing big to discuss. Penelope and John never thought their days could grow to be this boring, and even more surprisingly, they never thought they would hate it so much. Granted, they did not wish for the alternative.

Penelope seemed to be distracted, or rather interested, in this woman and her son. She saw her struggle most days, seeming to be alone with a four-year-old boy. This was tough enough, but one whose hearing was impaired; now that was a challenge she could not relate to.

Her heart pulled her towards them, wishing to offer help but fearing it would be taken the wrong way, for she was not one to have the standing to give advice. But Penelope was never one to ignore a person in need, especially someone she could actually help.

The woman began to softly cry, as she fought to capture her young sons' attention who wished to run away.

"Honey, you coming?" Tom asked Penelope, as she stood there with one hand in her overalls and the other in his hand. He moved towards their home, not sure what was keeping her.

"Y-yeah, just a minute. I'll meet you at home."

Tom nodded back with a curious look on his face. He signaled for John and Lily who were running around with Daisy in the general direction of home, not in any rush to get ready for bed.

"Please, honey. I can't show you what I want if you won't look at me," the woman said.

Penelope approached the woman with a kind smile as if trying to physically show she wasn't there to judge, but to maybe help. The woman smiled as an automatic response, but she was obviously preoccupied by her son.

Penelope turned to the boy who was thrashing about trying to get out of his mom's grip, but he stopped suddenly, distracted by the new person in front of him.

Penelope smiled at him and grabbed one of the flowers he had been so fixated by before. This was no surprise to Penelope, for they were a gorgeous shade of pink, one she tried most days to replicate.

The boy stretched his hands towards it as she got down on her knees, holding the flower in her hands and giving it a sniff. She then pushed it towards him to do the same. He smiled curiously at it and then began to sniff the flower like Penelope had done.

Penelope then put it behind her ear, took it off and put it behind his, to which he smiled, and she smiled back.

Penelope signed to the young boy a soft hello, surprising the mom she had not been introduced to yet.

"My father was hearing impaired," Penelope told the mom, who nodded in understanding.

"Is he here?" she asked, hopefully.

Penelope kept smiling at the young boy, waiting a moment before she responded. "He wasn't that lucky."

The woman stood there, unsure of what to say, not that there was anything that could be said in this type of situation, so she introduced herself instead.

"I'm Mia, and this little rascal is Parker," she said, finally getting his attention.

She signed to him that it was time to go home. His frustration at this request was quite present, making both Penelope and Mia laugh to themselves, both being mothers.

"I'm Penelope. I have a daughter around the same age, Lily, and a son, John, who is a bit older. If Parker would ever like to do a play date, we are just passed the dining hall, in the green bungalow with the multicolor chimes out front."

Mia smiled and nodded that that would be nice.

Penelope signed, "We have a dog; do you like dogs?"

Parker smiled very bright and signed an excited, "Yes."

"Tomorrow?" Mia asked.

"Sounds great," Penelope responded, signing goodbye to Parker before they started to head home.

They walked off in the other direction, leaving Penelope happy for them for being here but also saddened, as she reflected on her own misfortunes in that area. But just like everything else to do with that 'world', she had grown numb to its horror. One had to to survive, really.

She picked another flower and sniffed it, smiling as she admired its beauty. She walked back home slowly, putting her hands in her pockets casually, smiling at the those passing by her.

You have no idea how lucky you are to be here, she thought to herself.

She learned over the few months of being in Kairos that most people in this community had lived here for quite some time. In fact, they were quite shocked to see new visitors, and not in a good way. It seemed that they didn't like the reminder that there were others out there trying to escape, while they hid away in 'paradise'. It was a pain that Penelope wasn't getting used to. She wanted to do something about it — in time. They were still new, after all.

*

A year had passed, but in Kairos time seemed to move a lot slower than usual. Having little to do had that effect.

Penelope was finding her normal interests were lacking the joy they used to have, when it became the only thing she could do. Tom had run out of books to read, and to his disdain, he wasn't much of a writer, and nor was anyone in Kairos that he had met.

"I don't know why they have a library if they don't have any books," he said, frustrated, one night over dinner. He grabbed another roll from the breadbasket, supplementing his frustration through a couple extra pounds.

"I know, dear. I hate to say it, but I'm bored, and Kairos could use some work. I mean, don't get me wrong; it's great. It's just... lacking. At least in the city we could 'sneak' things of knowledge. We have the freedom but nothing to really do with it," Penelope said with a guilty voice.

They knew it was silly and unreasonable to ask for more, but it didn't stop them from wanting it. They would never wish to go back to the city — the fear and the lack of control — and they were the lucky few who were able to secretly avoid the cure. So they knew it wasn't right to complain about Kairos in comparison to what they had before, but that was the thing about dreaming of escape. It builds up and nothing can live up to it. Penelope and Tom were experiencing just that. They finally had freedom but not enough to be free. This led to boredom very quickly. They were grateful, obviously, but bored all the same.

It didn't help that they both grew up before Meno. They had memories of what life was like, and as amazing as Kairos was in comparison to the city, it was nothing compared to how the world used to be: vast and full of wonder; road trips of discovery; different cultures to experience and admire; beauty of difference everywhere. They had the ability to be different here in Kairos, but they still lived within borders of a woodsy sanctuary.

When you knew you had boundaries, it didn't matter how far they stretched; they quickly felt like they were encroaching in on you if all you sought was freedom. In some way this explained why the people of Kairos were less affected by their limitations. They didn't realize they had any.

Penelope longed most days to see the ocean once again, just that through everything, it still remained — just as vast and just as beautiful.

One day we will take them there... when it's safer to do so. She convinced herself of this regularly, not sure if it would ever be safe enough to do so.

"You scheduled for harvesting tomorrow, or maintenance?" Tom asked Penelope, moving on, feeling better having voiced his guilty frustrations and to find he was not alone.

With a mouth full of pasta, Penelope nodded yes, begging the look from Tom that read 'And which of the two options is it?'

Penelope laughed. Her mouth now empty, she responded, "I'm scheduled to help fix the leak in the medicine wing. You, honey?"

In Kairos they weren't required to do anything, but it was highly encouraged. They wouldn't stop pestering you to do so, and you wouldn't have access to the spoils of said effort if you didn't. They figured it made sense, but it did lead to some not so enjoyable tasks. That being said, it was something to do to stop the boredom.

Being relatively new, Penelope and Tom wanted to make a good impression, so they took the not-so-desirable jobs, hoping to show it was a good thing that they were there. No matter their contempt for how Kairos was managed, it was nothing compared to the tirade in the city.

Penelope took any and every job that allowed her to be outside. There was a particularly notable day in which Penelope was fixing a leaky roof at the mess hall when it was raining, and she waved and smiled at passersby, without nothing thicker than a hoody and jeans to cover her. Her hair was a complete mess, and her grin was so wide it almost looked sarcastic. There was lots of whispering. All Penelope could make out through the thundering rain and distance between her and two little, old ladies passing by was the words 'crazy' and 'woman'. She imagined they were strung together.

This, of course, made Penelope chuckle as she embraced the rain while she worked. Tom, on the other hand, was not so fond of unruly elements that presented themselves on any given day. He chose jobs providing a bit of shelter when the days where less then predictable. Luckily for him, the past month had showed nothing but sun.

"I signed up for boundary check. I swear, all they have us do is just stand there for hours, but it gives me an idea of what our perimeters look like, and that's oddly not comforting at all; yet I feel the need," Tom said with a chuckle, and it seemed as if he did not really find it that funny after all.

Penelope shook her head. "I know. I did that last week. It's not nearly enough. We should be training in defense, structurally and physically. And after we do that, we should maybe send out people for supplies or information; find a way to take back the city."

Penelope said this with confidence and anger, never liking the idea of sitting back while others were hurting and while her brother was missing. *Stop thinking of that,* she tried convincing herself.

She still found herself broken without her brother there, blaming herself, wishing to act, and in her mind she thought she had the means to do something. She had the desire and the understanding, but not quite the manpower, yet. To her, though, this was more than enough means. For it was more than most had in the city — consciousness of the imprisonment.

"Just give it some time, dear. They will come around. They are just afraid, and honestly, so am I," Tom said, feeding Lily some mashed butternut squash.

"I know, but this doesn't feel like fear, this feels like laziness," Penelope said honestly, her guilty conscience pressing further into her decision making.

"Fear often does; fear of doing anything at all. Fear of Meno is perfectly understandable. Look what they have done to our society; what we are forced to do. Meno knows the power of fear, and that's why they created the cure in the first place — to stop it. From their own fear of repercussions on the human race. We just need to come up with a plan and take our time settling in here," Tom pressed, trying to calm Penelope down — a big task if there ever was one.

"I know, Tom, but doesn't it bother you that if we were to be attacked today, we wouldn't be able to defend ourselves? At least, not enough? This type of fear that everyone has in Kairos is understandable, I get that. But unfortunately, it's not safe, and it can't be acceptable with the amount of people involved."

Tom sighed and sat back in his chair. He completely understood where his wife was coming from, and though she made a good point, he found it hard to admit that he felt himself becoming like them; just as fearful; just as blindly comfortable. In this moment he was thankful for her strong will; not the experiences that built them, but the backbone they needed to survive.

"You're right, dear, when the time is right, though, okay?" Tom pressed, urging her to take it easy, thinking that the rest of the town might not feel as kindly to her blatant criticism.

Penelope brushed his words off and replied, "When the timing is right," thinking to herself, *Who knows when that will be.*

"Anyway, we should head to the town council; its nearly time for the weekly meeting," Tom said.

They both rolled their eyes, knowing there was nothing really to gain from them.

"Right, well, unless anyone else has anything to add to tonight's proceedings, I think we can wrap up," Don, the appointed head of the town council, said, leaning back in his chair with a soft sigh that was granted from sitting in a wooden and uncomfortable chair for hours, like the rest of them.

The remaining hair on his head was white, and his stomach protruded noticeably, like most of those in Kairos, from growing too comfortable in their infectious bubble.

The people in the room reacted with the same feeling that was expelled from Don's sigh, as everyone got up to leave the small, wooden town hall, proceeding in the same fashion of nonchalant behavior. That was, of course, besides Penelope. She sat there, her hands unable to keep still, with Tom looking at her, hoping that she wouldn't do what he thought she might.

She had been fighting that voice in her head for so long, the voice that Tom had told her to silence for now. The pessimistic, scared voice in her head that feared their lack of fear would ruin this society, that they would not survive if they were to be attacked, which could happen any day now. Like sitting ducks ready for the picking, should they wish to dismantle them. She needed to do something, or this would be all ripped from her hands.

I can't let that happen again.

It felt to Penelope like they were just buying time here. Why didn't they ever talk about where they came from? Why didn't they make safety measures their number one priority? Surely none of them wanted to be cured and taken back. They wouldn't be here and have gone through this if they weren't certain about keeping as far away from them as they possibly could.

Tom tightened his hand on Penelope's knee. Lily was on his lap, and John was sitting on the other side of Penelope, both too young to quite understand what was going on, but happy to be included.

He tightened his grip as a simple and soft reminder to Penelope to be careful about saying anything. In his eyes they were still guests here, and if they so wished, they could force them out. It was something he had tried to voice to her many times, and it would be much worse than smiling at their hidden intentions.

Penelope, on the other hand, didn't see it that way. Subtlety and hiding her opinions to appease others had never been her way. Tom was much better at trying to see it from other people's perspectives, whereas Penelope was better at saying it how it was. They had both agreed years ago to agree to disagree with these topics of difference. Each secretly admiring the other's strength of understanding.

She squeezed his hand softly back as an acknowledgment that his opinion had been heard, but she had been quiet for months, years, and nothing had changed. She had waited for assurance that they were taking this seriously, that they would not just bend over should they be faced with a fight, and to Penelope this wasn't a matter of if, but when.

"Uh, excuse me; sorry, everyone. May I—" Penelope spoke, causing everyone who was getting ready to leave to stop and look curiously at the strange, new woman who stopped them from getting to bed.

Don, looking confused and annoyed, ushered for her to continue as he sat back down in his chair reluctantly.

"My name is Penelope, for those who I haven't been formally introduced to..."

No one said anything. They just continued to look over to her, with Mia smiling at her in reply.

"This is my husband, Tom."

Tom ushered a hand in the air as his way of saying hello.

"And of course, my daughter, Lily, and son, John. We are relatively new here, as you all know. And we, like I'm assuming most of you, are very happy and count ourselves lucky to be here. I will take my newness into consideration. Maybe I'm just more fearful, but I can't help but worry, or rather wonder — for my safety, for my family, for all of us — so pardon mean if this is a trivial question, but may I ask the council what safety measures we have in place?"

No one said anything, but the room felt eerily quiet. Penelope felt the temperature around her drop, and she felt that she wasn't going to particularly like the next words that came out of Don's mouth, though she sadly had already assumed what the answer would be.

Don looked to his fellow council members. They whispered softly to each other, leaving Penelope standing there unsure of how to hold her hands, so she put them in her pockets to prevent them from swinging at her sides.

A mousy-sounding woman, Terry, with her greying, wispy hair in a tight bun, sitting next to Don on the council, spoke up to answer the question as Don seemed out of his wheelhouse.

"What do you mean, dear?"

Penelope didn't think it was such a complicated question, and the fact that it seemed to make them at a loss for words showed her exactly how bad this was.

"If Meno did invade and try and take us back to the city, what would be the measures to stop them from doing so?"

Silence filled the room, and from the look on everyone's faces, she had clearly somehow over-stepped the line.

"W-we don't like to talk about *them,*" Terry said, clearing her throat uncomfortably. She ran her fingers over her necklace that was inlaid with something that sparkled if you looked at it from the right angle.

Penelope chuckled softly thinking that this must be a joke. But as she looked around at all the other residents who all of a sudden seemed to be very captivated by an invisible movie playing on the ceiling, the floor or anywhere, really, avoiding her gaze, she realized it was far from it. Except for Tom, who looked at her with a face that could only be summed up with two words, 'The fuck?'

"I understand how horrible Me—" She quickly stopped herself from saying the whole name. "*They* are. But that's exactly *why* we need to talk about them. And excuse my bluntness, but we can't forget what they did, and we have to take them into account with every decision we make."

"Frankly, dear, we wouldn't know where to start," Don said, honestly.

Penelope was shocked, and in some way, comforted, because they were being honest, and the lack of defense was not because of not caring but because they didn't know how. At least that's what she hoped. It wasn't because they didn't want to, it was because they didn't know where to start.

She wondered how long these people had been here and how they had gone so long without a disturbance from the city; could it be generations? How far back did Kairos's establishment go?

"I'll think on it. I'll come up with something," Penelope said, before the words stuck into her mind.

"O-okay, then. Well, we look forward to your ideas next week," Don said, obviously lying.

They all looked like she had pulled the soft, comforting blanket off their shivering shoulders as they now stood in the snow like they expected her to ask for a thank you. They all scoffed, as Penelope turned around to Tom who was now standing holding Lily in his arms and holding John's hand.

"Well, honey, not really the best way to make friends, but I'm sure they'll thank you for it eventually," he said with a sarcastic tone, making them both laugh.

"This is worse than I thought, Tom," she said in a more serious fashion.

"I know, but hey, think of it this way. Maybe this just means they aren't as broken as you," he said with a wink, to which she smacked him softly on the shoulder, making him laugh.

"Thank god, though I doubt it. They wouldn't be here if they had it easy before. But honestly, it's good thing we came — these people need a wake-up call," Penelope said harshly, as she began walking with Tom and their kids.

"Wake-up call or just a reminder? A punch to the face can wake someone, no question, but it won't bring them to head your advice; just think about it," Tom said, kindly.

Penelope stuck her tongue out in reply.

They exited the hall with what little residents were left. They were lingering and talking not so quietly in corners, every now and again looking over in Penelope and Tom's direction. It was quite obvious what was so important to discuss that it couldn't wait until they got home.

Penelope just smiled in their direction and waved. Tom bumped her shoulder softly as he began to walk next to her with their kids, as another soft, friendly reminder to play nice. It was something Penelope wasn't the best at. As Tom had put it many times before, though, 'This is a tight community; we don't have room to make enemies. We have nowhere else to go.'

Penelope knew this and tried very hard to remind herself of this, but it made her sick to her stomach, like getting a copper taste on her tongue just before throwing up.

She felt a tug on her overalls. John was wanting to be picked up in his sleepy state, so Penelope picked him up and he sank into his mom's comforting, warm and strong arms. He fell asleep quickly, lost in her soft, long curls that smelled like a mixture of lavender and old paint that had crusted on to the hair she had missed from placing in a messy bun last painting session.

"Come on, it's way past your guys' bedtime," Penelope said.

She followed Tom who was carrying Lily, and smiled at passersby in the most genuine way she felt she could muster. She tried her best to not appear sarcastic with her smile, though she doubted it came off as genuine as she hoped. If she was honest with herself, it was, in fact, closer to being sarcastic in its nature. She tried her hardest to be understanding, to not judge these people, having not truly known what they had gone through, but she couldn't help but be annoyed with them. In her eyes, they were being selfish and naïve. They couldn't just sweep this problem under the rug and pretend it wasn't there. She worried that they could one day repeat these horrors if they allowed themselves to forget, or worse, she feared they truly didn't know how bad it really was out there. How long had it been since someone had found their way here to Kairos?

It made the hair on her arms stand up, just thinking the one sentence she feared to even voice in her own head.

Did they even know who Meno really was and what was happening out there? Or even worse — what Penelope feared was true —did they even want to know?

*

Exactly two years and thirty-five days in the past

Back in the city, it was quiet like it always was. It was so quiet that on any given night it was normal for the crickets to be causing a disturbance, but not here. The sheer absence of noise would make any sane person a little crazy. However, something about the way the lawns were so manicured, the cars were all exactly the same shade of grey and everyone's lights went off at exactly eight-thirty p.m, would ensure the belief that this wasn't exactly a community that held much sanity to begin with. Though it didn't seem as if it was in their control to be aware, in the first place.

At twelve fifteen, one groggy and grey-hue covered resident was found doing something very out of character, for he would normally be sleeping without a hitch; he was happy, after all. Tonight, though, he sat up from his bed, as a crack between his beige-colored curtains that opened up to the street, allowed for him to be blinded by a bright, yellow light. He walked over, separated his blinds to find his neighbors all doing something similar. He watched, confused, as an odd-looking vehicle rumbled down the street and off into the distance. Without a second thought, he reached down to his rotary phone that was conveniently placed by his window and watched as his fellow neighbors did the same. Surely they must have seen the same thing and come to the same conclusion — the desire to help.

The phone rang twice before a kind, yet stern-spoken woman answered.

"Good evening, how may I assist you today, sir?"

The man cleared his throat softly as he continued to stare at the now-empty driveway of resident six-two, forty. "Good evening. I would like to report a disturbance. I think one of my neighbors needs assistance."

The woman paused for a moment, allowing for the man to hear a clinking of machinery in the background, and a distant ring.

"Of course, sir, that is very kind of you to inform us. What seems to be the matter they need assisting with?"

"I don't think they are sleeping okay; they just left their residence."

The woman paused even longer. Footsteps in the background came rushing through the phone, the man simply stood there, waiting for a response.

"Thank you very much, sir. We will come and see how we can help them. What is the address, sir?"

"Sixty-two, forty Plum Avenue."

"Thank you very much, sir. We do appreciate your concern for your neighbor's well-being, and we have just dispatched some peace officers to check in on them."

"Wonderful; thank you."

"It is my pleasure. I'd like to ask you a few questions, sir, if that's all right."

"Of course."

"How are you feeling tonight, sir?"

The man paused only momentarily before he responded with a smile on his face. "Very happy, thank you."

"Wonderful, and how would you rate the quality of this service today?"

"Ten out of ten, of course."

"I'm so happy to hear that, sir. Well, no need to fret any longer; you did the right thing. Now, why don't you go get some rest, and don't forget your appointment tomorrow with your doctor."

"Looking forward to it. Goodnight."

"Goodnight, sir."

He closed his blinds, watched his neighbors do the same, got into his bed and fell blissfully asleep.

It didn't take long for the authorities to make it to the residence of sixty-two, forty Plum Avenue, and to their dismay, it was indeed absent of its residents.

"I guess we found who was poisoning our residents," one of the peace officers said to the other, as they concluded that the house was completely abandoned, and in a rush.

"Yup, time to call the director. I want him to see this for himself. I don't want to be the one to tell him."

"Ten four."

The lieutenant standing beside his captain turned his head to the right to talk into his radio which had an angry-sounding voice booming through it. They both rolled their eyes and proceeded to sit on the stoop of the house, waiting for him to get there.

"How far do you think they'll get?" the lieutenant asked his captain, as they sat staring out at the perfectly manicured cul-de-sac.

"No one makes it past Kairos; I doubt they will."

Chapter Six

Three hundred and sixty-five days seemed like a long time when you thought of every second that passed in between them, and even more when you had nothing worthy of filling that time with. Luckily for the people of Kairos, time had actually passed quickly; so quick, in fact, that days had passed into years as it slipped out of their desired hands. They pressed every day for more time, and what they got in return was seven years of continuous training, development and expansion, since Penelope and Tom had arrived. It was still nowhere close enough to infiltrating the city like they wished to — like Penelope wished to. Tom agreed, but he was less enthusiastic about it. To be fair, though, this was in comparison to Penelope, someone who could clearly come off as obsessed, for reasons only Tom understood. It worried him every day, but he knew there was no stopping her, and for now, at least, they weren't able to act on their theories of attack. When they could, then he'd be worried — *very* worried.

Penelope had succeeded in convincing the council to allow her to try to make changes, after she had spread the fear in the once-blissfully happy citizens. She had left such a strong copper taste in their mouth that they gave her the means to try just so she could get rid of it and put the fear on her shoulders alone. Then they could go back to living their lives as normally as possible.

They didn't realize she was going to run with it. The barracks had been strengthened, monitored and put on a rotation of protection. It was a *real* rotation of protection, another point she made very clear.

Penelope wasn't in this to make friends, but she said many times to Tom when he brought this up at night, "Do you think anyone worth a damn accomplished something by people-pleasing? I think not."

This always made Tom laugh and instilled in himself the love he had for this stubborn, strong-willed woman.

"Just as long as you don't mind fighting that battle alone is all I'm saying," Tom reciprocated.

Penelope gave him a questionable look.

"Just as long as you don't mind *us* fighting that battle alone," Tom quickly corrected, pulling himself out of some quickly rising water.

Penelope nodded in a way that read 'That's right,' causing Tom to roll his eyes and laugh.

"As powerful as an artist and a teacher are..." Tom paused, expecting a response from Penelope, but he had an expression on his face that told her to let him finish. "I don't think it would hurt to have some help from someone who is trained for this; if there is anyone in Kairos, that is."

Penelope paused, crossed her arms and then replied, "Fair enough; we start looking tomorrow."

She walked away to finish brushing her teeth, leaving Tom thinking, '*We?*'

She was lucky to find an old, naval officer in Kairos who, after her prepared speech of duty and responsibility coupled with her relentless tirade of annoying the man, finally gave in. He finally agreed to help, appreciating her gumption, and offered his services to instruct on combat as best he could in his older age that mixed with years in Kairos with his feet up. Penelope, on the other hand, couldn't be more ecstatic about his experience and was ready to utilize every bit of it that she could. She would take anything she could get, and he was the least short straw she seemed to be grasping.

Penelope was instructed by the council that she could use their resources to protect and defend Kairos, but they were very specific about not extending that to outside the community. They feared that it would lead the city to attack, and as she had so softly showed them, they wouldn't be prepared for that.

Penelope understood and accepted this but that was years ago, and no matter how many times she brought it up at weekly council meetings, they didn't change their minds. She was so persistent that her hand could be seen most nights going unnoticed in the crowd, assuming her desire to rest her arm was less than their stubbornness to ignore it. It usually came to a tie.

Seven years had passed and things were better, but Penelope was restless and quite frankly tired of being told what she could and couldn't do.

John and Lily, however, found themselves adjusting quite well. Parker was a dear friend of theirs now, and Penelope and Tom always knew they would thrive a lot more here than they did in the city. To Tom's disappointment, they took after their mother in wishing to spend every and any moment outside. They did, nonetheless, reserve a few hours at night to listen to their father read to them and talk about philosophy. That was, of course, after they came home one night laughing and covered in mud, to find their kind father sitting on the porch and staring off in the distance with the saddest look they'd ever seen. Whether this was intentional or not didn't matter to John and Lily. They made sure to save time to enjoy what their father loved in life. In fact, John found, as he got older, a love for these conversations — these moments connecting with his father — mainly because he'd never seen him happier.

One peaceful night in their little bungalow, Penelope was in the kitchen teaching Mia the secret to her chicken noodle soup, which just happened to be drinking wine and letting it do its thing. Lily was curled up with Daisy, using her mom's paint set to make a creation that would remain a fixture on the wooden floors for years to come. John and Parker were sitting on the balcony with Tom, going over a particularly fascinating book Tom had brought from the city. It was one, he told the boys, that might have been the most important one he saved.

John and Parker looked at each other with questioning eyes, as Tom was always saying that the book he had in his hands was important. So what made this one in particular special?

"It's not particularly what's in the book, it's what the book causes." Tom started the conversation in speech and sign language with such intensity that the two young boys laughed, thinking he was joking around.

Tom laughed back at their response. "I'm serious, boys. It is extremely important. It, to me, brings up the one thing that could crumple the very fabric of Meno."

Now he had their attention.

"It insights the desire to question," Tom said, in a mysterious and exciting tone.

John rolled his eyes at this. "Oh, we know that. You and Mom have been telling us, since we could breathe, to question."

Parker signed. "We all know."

"Yes, but do you know why?" Tom pressed.

The boys looked at each other and collectively seemed to agree on an answer.

"Because of Meno," John replied easily.

"Nope. Meno works to take your questioning away, but that's not why it's important."

The boys looked confused, as if this was a trick question that they weren't going to get right.

"Oh, and let me guess; that book tells us why?" John said with a laugh, making Parker laugh as well.

"It highlights its importance, yes. All philosophy and all knowledge from science to math to the arts and everything in between, stems from the simple idea. Curiosity. This is what makes us human," Tom pressed.

"So why did Meno think it right to take it away?" John asked his father honestly, which caused Tom to smile.

"That's a very good question. I think that on some level they genuinely thought they were helping us. We didn't have enough answers to the problems we had created, and our society was darkened by this. They thought, on some desperate level, that there was no hope for our future and wished to give us a break. The other part of it is that they were too afraid of not having answers, or finding any, so they wished to lessen the pressure. I don't imagine they expected to give it up entirely; something like that happens over time. It was in the end, unfortunately, easier."

"Not to agree in any sense with Meno, but if they removed our need to question because there were no answers, isn't that okay? I mean, what is the point of questioning if you will never find an answer?" John asked, sincerely.

Tom was still smiling. He felt he was getting somewhere.

"Yes, the answer is what drives us to question in the first place, right? In the simplest terms, a question is when we see something and we wonder what it is, or how it functions, or why it functions in that way. And the whole point, as you stated, is to find the *answer*. Oh, it's a tree that provides fruit for us to consume and sustain our existence, or to provide shade on a hot day; maybe it will bring comfort by its soft flowing branches and a perfect spot to sit under and read" Tom said, as he stood up and put his hand on their apple tree stretching over their deck.

"But now imagine that before you were given the chance to even wonder, you were given the answers. You walk up to a tree, and I tell you, 'Hey this is a tree — it provides sustenance.' Therefore, there was no instance of you thinking for yourself or choosing what it means to you.

"Should be fine. I just saved you the trouble of figuring it out. Now, what if I gave you the *wrong* information, such as that a tree does nothing but provide some shade on a hot day, and I denied, or rather removed, your ability to harvest from that tree. Years go by and I pass away. You've passed along this information, but someone asks you what these red things that grow on its branches are. And you don't have the answers. Or maybe the tree dies out because you didn't know how to keep it alive. Or even worse, you never knew what an apple even was. Questioning is what keeps us alive. It keeps us aware of the world around us; it gives us a reason to survive, to live.

"Sure, you might question things, looking to find answers, but that's not really why you ask. You ask the questions because you had a spark of curiosity. You thought for yourself and wished to understand. That doesn't go away after you find an answer — it just moves on to a new one.

"In my opinion, our society has always been built off far too many facts and not enough theories.

"Nothing about life is for certain, and the second we try to legitimize our beliefs in stone, we forget the reason why we started to question in the first place. We forget that we, at one point or another, had no answers; that being human isn't about being intelligent enough to know, but wise enough to question. All knowledge and all education derives from this simple act of curiosity. Without it, we are limited to so much of this world and that of our expansion as a society. This is the root of humanity."

Tom, proud of himself for making a fair point, grabbed an apple off the tree he was leaning on and took a big bite.

"Someone could say this is poisonous. Sure, they could be right, and I could die from trying, but that is the great thing, the vital thing of humanity. We are a perfect mix of stupidity, curiosity, and drive. Without all three, we'd still be living in caves with barely any thought process to think of."

John looked at his father with a look that read, 'My father is either a genius or a little mad.' *I guess he could be both, but he does, in fact, have a point.*

"Tom! I have not been cooking dinner for hours for you to spoil it with an apple!" Penelope shouted from the kitchen window, making Mia laugh.

Tom laughed too. "Are you drinking wine without me? That's my favorite part of the cooking process," he joked, moving towards the kitchen, stopping only to hand John the philosophy book bound tightly in brown leather and string.

"John, I want you to have this," he said with a smile. "I know it backwards and forwards, and if I need to borrow it, I know where you live." He winked and smiled, to which John reciprocated.

He then opened the front page and pointed to a title in the syllabus. It read in gold letters:

'The Meno Puzzle'

"I'd pay specific attention to this chapter," Tom said with a smile, as if letting his son in on a grand secret.

The word Meno rang through John's mind. He was perplexed that its origin was in the same book his father held so tight.

"Thanks, Dad, I love it," John replied.

He watched his father walk through the open front door and into the kitchen, where he was handed a fairly large glass of wine. The kitchen was filled with such laughter, one could almost feel the warmth radiating out of it.

Parker then turned to John. "May I take a look?" he signed, referring to the book.

John chuckled. "Of course."

Chapter Seven

One year Later

"Oh, I'm going to throw up," Tom said in the shower, as Penelope brushed her teeth and chuckled.

"Might help if you do," she said with a soft cackle.

"Thanks so much," Tom said, laughing back. His nerves calmed slightly from the light-heartedness of the conversation. "What if they don't like me?" he continued, feeling silly for even asking.

"Not possible. Besides, you're the teacher and you're in charge. If they don't like you, who cares?" Penelope replied, to which Tom opened the shower curtain and stared at her.

"I love you, honey, but you'd make a terrible teacher."

Penelope turned around and splashed him with water from the sink, making him laugh.

"Ass," she replied, as she smiled and continued brushing her teeth.

Tom's weak stomach was coming from something specific; he was anticipating his first day teaching in Kairos. It was something he had longed for since they got here —it had only taken him eight years.

Nevertheless, Tom was excited just the same, and in some way, more so, as it had been eight years since he had last taught, and his lecture was written for him. He had always dreamed of this day, never really assuming it would actually happen. Yet, his chance was here, and Tom had finally been given the ability and trust to begin instruction. He was growing bored of simply reading what little they had in Kairos and trying his hand at writing in his spare time, something he had grown a strong detest and self-loathing to. He could barely contain his excitement when he was given approval to be the new instructor in their youth program in Kairos. He had shown Penelope his writing over the years in Kairos, needing an intellectual release, knowing he himself detested his own words.

She had smiled kindly which he read right through and threw it in the closest bin.

"You are a harsh critic," Penelope had said, as she tutted, pulled it out and put it in the draw for safe-keeping.

"My dear, I'm not, it's just that bad," Tom replied, making her chuckle.

"No, it's not. It's a piece of you. That's the best part of everything," Penelope replied, sitting on John's lap as he sat back in his office chair.

He chuckled before giving her a kiss. "Why, thank you, my love, but honestly, I miss teaching."

"I know, my love. Soon, yes? Keep fighting for it, like I do with the council."

Tom laughed. "Maybe a little less enthusiasm for me. I actually want to become a teacher at some point, not piss people off," he said with a wink, making Penelope punch him softly while chuckling back.

"Yes, well, I've made progress, so who's to say it isn't working."

"This is true. I'll try," he said softly, making Penelope smile.

Something Tom said must have worked; that or the 'teacher' they had was eager for help, because within a few short months since Tom had spoken up, he was a day away from his first lecture, exhausted from a day in the fields.

As he began getting dressed for bed, having finished his shower with the achievement ringing over him that he indeed did not throw up, and was now laying out his outfit for the next morning multiple times, he gave his mind time to do what it did best when he was nervous — overthink.

He quickly realized that he could potentially be the most traveled and versed person in Kairos on literature and education. Having been a teacher in the city, he had access to lots of information — secretly, that was, with its many risks of being discovered.

But so far he enjoyed Kairos more, because he was not only able to educate himself fully, but he was now able to really teach his students. The content was endless, and he felt invigorated. If only he had crammed more in his bags when leaving and jotted down more in his trusty notebook. But all the same, he finally had more minds to mold and bounce ideas and concepts off.

Oh my god we can debate! he thought excitedly to himself. Education in the city served one simple purpose and it made Tom's blood boil; its purpose being training —training for professions that served the city and not its people. There was no furthering one's mind's eye or finding oneself through discovery. Now everything had changed, and for once he could share it with people other than his family. He might actually find someone who shared his love for literature. John and Lily would read books with him and engage in light conversation about the works he longed to unravel, but being still young, they would on most occasions roll their eyes at what they called his constant rambles. Penelope would kindly correct them, saying it was called 'constant inquisitiveness'.

"Which is a great trait to have, mind you."

Tom could, of course, talk to Penelope about this stuff, but she was more of a private contemplator, and he longed for debate. Even more so, the teacher in him longed for that spark he always dreamed of in a student or peer when he taught them something so profound in their young eyes that it changed them forever, gave them hope and made them into the person they would grow up to be.

He knew, of course, that this was a lot of pressure to put on a child, so he hid this dream to himself, hoping that one day he would be pleasantly surprised by his own teaching skills.

The day of his first class, he woke up in a sweat having not slept very well. He had been so excited about the prospect of it, he hadn't fully realized the severity of what this meant. He was the first teacher in Kairos with latest information to teach, and even more so, the first in a very long time who didn't seem afraid to explore where the city had gone horribly wrong. Too afraid, or maybe intentional in keeping children from the horrors around them, the educators in Kairos, in Tom's opinion, had done them a serious disservice by keeping them in the dark.

This put a lot more pressure on him, and this was becoming very apparent this morning before his first lecture.

Penelope rolled over to hug him in a sleepy state, as she had been sleeping a little more restfully. In her groggy state, she curled into Tom's nook and asked, "Didn't sleep well, my love?"

Tom wrapped his arms around her, brushing her overgrown bangs out of her face, and gave her a kiss on the forehead. "You could say that."

"Well, that's normal. You always have trouble sleeping before a lecture," Penelope said, reassuringly.

"Yeah, but this time it's different. For once I'm afraid of not having *enough* information, of not living up to the hype."

Penelope chuckled softly to herself. "Tom, trust me. You definitely live up to the hype." She smiled and gave him a soft kiss, making him chuckle while holding her tighter.

"Well, as long as you think so, nothing else matters," Tom said softly, feeling a little bit better but still nervous as hell.

"I'm surprised the lovelies aren't up yet," Penelope said in a hushed voice, and as if they somehow heard her, she heard their voices coming from the other room.

"Mom, can you help me with my homework?"

"Dad, where's Daisy's leash? She has to go to the bathroom."

Tom chuckled. "You always jinx us," he said, tickling Penelope's sides as they both got up reluctantly, wishing they had more time in bed together.

Crisp bacon sizzled in the pan as Tom came over to Penelope and watched it with anticipation. He filled her recently empty coffee cup with copious amounts of fresh, dark roast coffee and gave her a kiss on the cheek. Holding a plate of freshly scrambled eggs, he went over to John and Lily who were waiting impatiently at the dining table.

"All right, who wants eggs!" Tom said, holding up the plate in his hand.

John and Lily replied with soft, groggy grunts, more awake once the eggs made their way around, as he plated up five plates of eggs.

"Here we go," he said, as he placed them down in front of their beaming faces. Daisy's being the most grateful.

Penelope came around with the finished bacon, the true star of the plate.

With everyone's breakfast being wolfed down with excitement, they all grabbed their stuff for the day: backpacks, tool bags, book bags and Daisy's to-go bag, as she was going for a day on patrol with Penelope.

Daisy even had her bandana on that Penelope had made. It read, in bright, red letters 'Protection Squad'. She wore it with pride every day on patrol. She sat by the door, ready for a day's work, giving all her family members a wet, sloppy kiss as they made their way out the door for the day. She then finally followed Penelope's lead as they headed to patrol duties.

Tom ushered John and Lily out the door, after making sure for the third time that they had everything, since he wasn't certain if he did. He stopped for a moment as Penelope gave them hugs and kisses, finishing with him.

"You'll do great, my love. And if you don't, I'll still love you," she said, with a soft laugh that was reciprocated.

"Thanks, hun. Have a peaceful patrol, yes?"

Penelope nodded as they headed in opposite directions.

Tom followed behind John and Lily who were in a deep conversation about some girl named 'Patty'. John was instructing Lily on what to do if she picked on her again. If Tom had been listening close enough and not been distracted by his own thoughts about his first lecture, he might have heard the words 'swift kick' and advised otherwise. He, of course, did not hear this. Instead, he kept drinking his coffee in his thermos and tried his best to appear together, as they were approaching more residents the closer they got to school.

Tom nodded and smiled softly at all the residents he happened to pass as he made his way to the center of Kairos, trying his best to not throw up.

"Good luck, Tom!" an older woman shouted, from where she was sitting on the front porch of one of the many bungalows they were passing along the way.

"Thank you, Jane!"

Tom wasn't sure if it was sincere or if his nervous energy was noticeable from a distance. Either way, he was not a fan of the attention.

A few minutes later they arrived at the education building right next to his classroom, and he dropped off John and Lily with the other rambunctious kids.

"See you later, Dad. Good luck. Just try not to throw up in front of the whole class, yeah?" John said, with a comforting shoulder pat and laugh.

Tom chuckled sarcastically as his way of saying 'Thanks, Son.' Tom gave him a hug before he ran off to meet up with his friend, Parker, who was sitting on the top of one of the benches in front of their classroom.

"Bye, Daddy!" Lily said, throwing herself into Tom's arms, making him expel a much-needed chuckle.

"Bye honey. Have a great day at school." Tom replied, with a final kiss to Lily's cheek and a wave in their direction, as they ran into the garden that had been converted into a day care center.

"Hey, Tom! How ya' doin? Am I mistaken or is today your first class?"

Tom turned around to see his friend, Pat, a man who looked like a professional bodybuilder but who, in fact, loved baking. Pat made the best bread in all of Kairos. He didn't have the biggest competition, but it was delicious all the same. His partner, Mike, used to be an officer in the city. He was muscley too, but not to Pat's scale, that's for sure.

"Hey, Pat! Yeah, was it that obvious?"

"I didn't want to say anything, but yeah, you do look a little pale," Pat said with a chuckle, making Tom laugh back.

"Yeah, and to think I begged for this day."

Pat chuckled. "You'll do great. I'll see you later."

"Thanks, take care," Tom replied, as Pat walked towards the bakery and Tom made his way slowly to his classroom.

Oh, good god, here we go.

*

This time of day was always beautiful in Kairos: people just starting their day with a few having started early, like those fixing the leaky roof of the mess hall, worried about the expected rain, so they got up particularly early.

Penelope waved to the workers as she passed by them with Daisy in tow. Having become increasingly more familiar with the people in Kairos, she smiled and waved when passing every resident on her way to the outskirts of their community.

Penelope was still unsure whether these smiles from everyone were entirely genuine or whether they were simply being civil due to the sheer size of their community —keeping the peace and all that. But Penelope knew, at least, that her smiles were genuine; for most of them, that was.

She skirted the line of annoying to some residents as she pushed for change and better protection, and with some of the more settled-in residents, this did not go over well. Settled in or fearful — they both did not approve of this change. But those who didn't fear in the community of Kairos thanked Penelope, like they had been waiting for someone to voice their same concerns but didn't feel they had the platform to do so.

Luckily for them, Penelope was kind, confident and self- assured.

This, however, was a classic nurture versus nature trait. She developed this after experiencing lack of control and lack of voice in the city. That would cause anyone to not care too much what others thought of their opinions but rather thankful for the ability to finally have them. She did find herself a little rusty in public. In her home with her family, she voiced her true self with small reservations of concern that they might be listening in somehow, not putting it past Meno.

But now, in public, she could choose to not smile if she didn't want to. That was significant. Still, there was anxiety rolled up in it.

Daisy being by her side helped, though — it always helped. Most of Penelope's successful interactions were initiated by Daisy's beaming face, something she would forever be thankful for. She would always regard her best days as spent with Daisy by her side.

Penelope had made it past most of the bungalows, the dining hall and multiple gardens interspersed throughout their compound, on their way to the far-right corner of the boarder. About fifteen minutes earlier, they had passed the last bungalow and entered a beautiful forest that filled the otherwise bare part of the compound. Penelope wondered whether it was bare out of protection, keeping their homes further from the walls that protected them, or if they assumed they'd have a larger community. Based upon the fact that they were shocked to see Penelope and her family, it gave the impression that their reach wasn't as far as they had hoped. That, or their objective had changed, and they were not as hidden as they imagined.

Either way, Penelope loved this part of the compound. It was one of the reasons she didn't really mind patrols. It was so peaceful here, except for the occasional group of residents walking through, or the class of children being taught by the river that flowed through on the right side of two protruding oak trees, making a beautiful collection of ecological examples to teach the children.

Daisy always loved it when they passed others in the forest — always a lover of people, especially kids — though she still found ways to entertain herself, following the lizards and flies scattering about with their larger movements.

Penelope got so much inspiration for her painting when she went on these patrols, that she kept a small notebook on hand to sketch down some inspiration. But it wasn't the same to draw the beauty around her in harsh, black ink, when the reason she was inspired was because of the vibrant colors around her.

If only I had a camera, she thought longingly to herself. Those, of course, were rare, and she hadn't seen one in over twenty years.

As she continued on her predetermined path, whose forest floor had been softened compared to that of the grass around it due to consistent travelers heading this way, she waved to the group of residents who were at its end.

They all waved or nodded in response and gave Daisy warmer greetings as she happily moved towards each of them, basking in their warm greetings with butt pats here and face rubs there and many, *many* tail wags in every direction.

"Good morning, everyone," Penelope said with a smile, to which they responded kindly back.

Pat, the baker, was a kind, brawny gentleman who used to be in the navy and now pursued what he really loved. His grey beard and bald head hid reminiscence of his younger ginger years.

He opened his backpack and pulled out a thermos, a water bottle, five cups and a dog bowl. He placed the dog bowl down and poured water in it, accompanied by licks of appreciation from Daisy who had quickly become their mascot and close friend. He then handed everyone a cup after he filled it with steaming, hot coffee. He received a special thanks from everyone, as they now always looked forward to Pat's delicious coffee before work.

He quickly became one of Penelope's favorite people in the community to work with, for no apparent reason at all. She stood there cupping the warm, delicious coffee in her hands on this misty, dew-filled morning.

"You're a saint, Pat, you really are," Penelope said with a smile, to which he tilted his hat as a kind response.

"Come over after shift. I have some bananas that need to be used. I'll send you home some fresh banana bread to give Mike. I know how much he loves it, and I still need to thank him for babysitting the kids last week."

"Aw, he'll love that. Thanks, Penelope," Pat said with a smile, as he continued to pet Daisy.

They all talked amongst themselves for a moment, letting the coffee wake them and resting momentarily after the trek through the community and woods to get there this morning.

"All right, Ryan, you were on early morning patrol, right?" Penelope asked softly, to which he nodded.

One or two gleeful residents had the 'lucky' task of waking up before sunrise to walk the length of one side of the fence to look for any problems they could work on for the day. The same occurred on the other four sides of the boarder, all meeting up around this time to discuss what they had found.

"Yeah, everything seemed relatively together, except on the far north side of the fence where our boarder lies, there was some wood that seemed to be corroded and in need of replacement."

Sherry, a woman about the same age as Penelope, with beautiful, darkened features spoke up next. "I'll go tell Henry in the lumber yard that we need a repair."

They all nodded as she finished her coffee, handed the cup to Pat with a thank you and began walking back towards the center of town.

"Any holes? In the fence?" Penelope asked, taking another swing of her coffee.

"Yeah, but it's technically in unit two's territory."

"Barnes, you want to come with me and see if unit two needs a hand fixing it?" Pat asked.

Barnes nodded with a sigh and handed their empty cup back to Pat. Penelope finished hers as well, putting it in Pat's bag with another thank you and placing Daisy's bowl in it too, since Daisy had finished her water and was now preoccupied by the treat Penelope had given her to eat.

Pat and Barnes took off to the left of the forests edge to see if they could lend a hand.

"What about any animals? Any problems?" Penelope pressed, picking up conversation with Ryan, the youngest man on patrol.

He wasn't much older than Penelope's son, John, with wavy blonde hair covering his otherwise bright eyes.

"Yeah, let me show you," Ryan said, putting his backpack on and heading towards the direction he seemed to have noticed something off, with Daisy and Penelope on his heels.

"I didn't think much of it at first, but the tracks were a little bigger than I've seen before, and I thought maybe you'd know what they were," Ryan said, embarrassed.

He wasn't a fan of not understanding things happening around him, but he learned very quicky that Penelope wasn't one to put anyone down for it; she just simply had more experience, being from outside of Kairos. Even if that was in a city, she was old enough to have grown up before the cure, and her parents had been big fans of the outdoors.

They approached the tracks, and Penelope was surprised at the size of them. They seemed to be the size of a bear, but not having a book on tracking, she couldn't be certain.

"It looks like it could be a bear footprint? Though I don't know the proper distinction, the size and the indentation seems right. How strange. I mean, there is a stream, so they have food, but this is pretty open forest with not much coverage, and I don't see too many rock protrusions for them to have a cave to sleep in," she said methodically, pressing her hand into the footprint and following its path with her eyes, as Daisy sniffed the ground, trying to be helpful.

A few yards away, barely visible, was a beautiful and barely-moving grizzly. Her heart quickened and she ushered for Daisy to sit, who did exactly that.

Penelope began to move towards it slowly, hand over her hunting knife, hoping she didn't have to use it.

"How many bears do you guys usually get here?" she asked quietly and in a concerned voice, as she approached the bear.

Ryan looked at her confused, hesitating before responding. "What's a bear?"

Right. Of course, Penelope thought to herself, feeling surprised every time that they didn't know of something that seemed so commonplace to her.

"This is a bear," Penelope said, approaching it.

It almost looked like it was in hibernation. She could see it breathing, and there were specks of blood on its fur. It did not even attempt to move when they approached.

You poor thing, she thought to herself, watching it softly stir, hand still on her knife just in case.

Ryan tilted his head as if to convey his confusion and then answered her original question, more wrapped up in her question than seeing a bear a foot away from where he was standing, as if this was a normal situation for him to find himself in. "A couple times a year; depends on the frequency of the burning."

Now Penelope was the one that was confused. "What burning?"

"Oh, of course it hasn't happened in a while — years in fact but the fires sometimes send animals into our grounds."

"Natural fires or...?"

"Oh, yeah, this happens every now and again. The city burns the forest down and the adjacent wildlife seem to lose it — get disoriented. This is just a patch job," he said, looking at the whole in the fence.

"Disoriented how?" Penelope asked, her curiosity peaked, still staring at the bear below her.

"I don't know; docile? Makes them easier to hunt, I imagine."

Penelope looked at the bear she was standing over. His eyes were glazed, and he was barely moving. Her heart ached for such beautiful creatures. She wished to put a hand on it but previous advice suggested otherwise, so she simply knelt down, looking for any signs of significant harm.

"We will move the bear to the other side of the fence and give it some jitter juice," Ryan said, taking a dropper full of blue liquid and handing it to Penelope.

Apparently they weren't too afraid of being maimed by the bear. Either that, or the bear really was harmless in this state.

"Molly, can you go tell Roy we have another breach again? We will need his help carrying this one out of the barrier," Ryan said to a woman who had just appeared for duty.

She nodded as if this was normal maintenance.

"What is it?" Penelope said with curiosity, staring at the liquid Ryan handed her.

"Oh, well, apparently before we had set barriers like we do today, Hubert, our head horticulturist, was off collecting in the forest and found the wildlife eating this blue flower. It seemed to be the only thing that survived the fires. I imagine that's why they kept eating it — got a taste for it, I reckon. Hubert, the kook that he is, thought it meant more than that, as he usually does. This time he was right. I'm not sure how, but apparently it helps them. It's got some kind of nourishment that gives them a boost. Not my area of expertise, if I'm honest. So he took some, turned it into a liquid and we put a couple drops in their mouth when we find them. It seems to do the trick when they become disoriented —

at least, slightly. They are gone in the morning when we go to check, so it must be doing something right. Either that, or they get up on their own," Ryan said, with a strong lack of interest on the subject.

Penelope laughed to herself in amazement as she gripped the vile tightly in her hand, afraid to let it go. "Where is this genius man? I must meet him," she exclaimed.

"Why?" Ryan asked, scratching his peach stubble, feeling that he had explained everything that needed to be explained.

Penelope kept staring at the bottle and replied softly, "I have many questions."

She knew how crazy she would sound if she voiced her thoughts, and yet she was quite certain they were on to something — something very important and overlooked — something that caused Penelope to smile.

*

Quite a few years passed at Kairos and much had changed. Whether it was for the better would depend on who you talked to. One citizen, in particular, in Kairos seemed to be a little antsy, or rather, hesitant, about every improvement made. It was as if he didn't want Kairos to get better, to be safer or to prosper.

He became so suspicious that people were starting to notice and they gained no comfort or understanding from confronting him. Fearing that he might be crazy or unhinged, his friends and colleagues began to press him for answers, which only drove him to quickly become a shut-in, for reasons they still didn't know. He began to only grant them with his presence on specific occasions. He stopped his late afternoon walks, coming out only when running out of supplies, and necessary council meetings; that was, when he didn't cancel last minute stating that he was feeling ill, yet the local doctor said he hadn't been by to see him. There were even whispers by citizens, stating in concern, that he had been seen going up and questioning others on happenings in the town and then scurrying away when groups began to form. Suffice to say, he was quickly growing a reputation as the kind, older man that people kept their distance from, and he was the main piece of gossip in such a small, boring community.

"Maybe he's losing it"

"Maybe he's afraid of being overturned as head council?"

"Maybe he ate too much Jaja root?"

All of these were speculations that Don never addressed, and his actions when he did appear in town only made their speculations more exuberant.

There was a knock on Don's door in the middle of the night. He ran over, looking concerned and erratic, and peered through the small crack provided between his curtain and window frame to see who could possibly be there at that time of night.

His eyes went wide, and to the visitor who was waiting impatiently outside, it sounded like something was knocked over and then hastily put back up before the door swung open.

The visitor looked questioningly at the disheveled man before him and then rolled his eyes before stepping back into Don's small garden.

"You broke our deal, Don," the director hissed, as Don cowered even further.

"Look, it wasn't me, okay. I didn't ask for this. I didn't want this!" he tried to say with confidence, but no one would buy that he was anything but terrified.

The director just stood there, staring at him as if he was an ant under a magnifying glass, not needing to say a word; He waited for him to squeal and say everything he needed to hear.

"Okay, okay. Stop looking at me like that, would you; it gives me the creeps," Don said, shaking off the chill he was now unpleasantly overcome with. "There are some newcomers. They wanted a change. They wanted to make it safer here, but I didn't think it was a problem—"

"You didn't think is right! Every matter of change I should be informed with. That was our arrangement," the director bellowed, as loud as he could, while they tried to stay hidden outside of Don's bungalow in the middle of the night.

The only light to be seen was at the far end of his housing corner, but it was quiet and still in Kairos, so they had to be quiet too.

The director didn't feel like he needed to yell to get his point across, but Don had a way of angering him to the point that it was hard to control his volume. Either he was going to shout or punch the man. Neither worked for him right then, so he stepped back and sighed to himself. In his best controlled manner, he tried to reestablish his point.

"Tell... me.... everything."

Don just softly nodded that he understood, before inviting the director inside, pouring him a large glass of whiskey and doing exactly as he was told.

Chapter Eight

Things happen sometimes, and we don't always know why. Every day we experience things, react...don't react. But sometimes, when we least expect it, things happen to us for a reason. Why?

That is one of those frustratingly normal acts of life. Serendipitous, some people like to call it.

For Penelope, on this very early morning in the Kairos barracks, this was not the case. There was a very specific reason for the events that were about to hit her like a ton of bricks.

She reached over in her groggy state and found that Tom had rolled further away than she would have liked. She scooted herself over to his side, pulling herself into him, breathing deep and inhaling his intoxicating scent. She had her arms wrapped around him tightly as he held her hands. They lay there, feeling content, happy to steal away these beautiful, perfect moments together when they didn't have to feed the kids or the dog or go do their part in their community. They could just lay there together, uninterrupted, half awake, half blissfully unaware.

Penelope was softly smiling as she pressed herself further into Tom, when suddenly she felt nothing. Startled and confused, she thought that somehow he must have scooted further away sleepily, but when she met the edge of the bed she quickly sat up, realizing he wasn't there.

Like a mirage she saw a faint glimmer of what she associated with Tom walking towards their bedroom door, and without opening it he went right through, fading into the open air. She sat up fully, in a panic. Her heart was pounding and her body was sweating as she ran from her bed, leaving through the adjacent door in their bedroom to their back garden.

It was dark all of sudden. Time and reality did not have a place in that moment, as fire ingulfed simultaneously around her and every building she could see. Distant screams rang all around her as Tom came running up holding John and Lily, who were both passed out. It gave her serious déjà vu, and yet it felt like she was experiencing it for the first time.

"Honey, take them, I'm going back for Daisy. I thought she was right behind me. Honey, quick, take the kids!" Tom said in a panic, while Penelope did just that.

She was terrified. She tried to wake John and Lily, but they barely moved. She felt for a heartbeat, thankful to feel two. She pulled them off to the side of their bungalow and away from the growing flames.

Tom ran into the house that was burning rapidly, as Penelope screamed for him and Daisy in the distance.

Penelope's screams weren't the only ones. Everyone in their community seemed to be experiencing the same thing. Screams of horror and fast-moving footsteps made it clear the whole community was being attacked.

Why is this happening? Her conscious tried to seek reason.

Why wouldn't it happen? Her pessimistic viewpoint crept in far too quickly.

We have to get out of here, quick, Penelope thought to herself, knowing she would never let her children go back to the city again.

She went to wake John and Lily forcefully and thought of going back in the house after Tom and Daisy, but for some unknown reason, her body moved like molasses, and her normal, level head was scattered.

Was it the smoke? Did they use the same fire they used on the animals? They wouldn't... *they would.*

Penelope wasn't the only one who was sluggish. She was witnessing people who seemed to be trying to flee, crawling past her.

Tom and Daisy. *They won't make it out,* Penelope thought in horror.

She began to crawl towards their house when suddenly Tom came blundering through carrying Daisy, who also seemed to be in a deep sleep.

Tom fell to his knees and laid Daisy between John and Lily.

The smoke was too heavy to see through and too heavy to try and talk. Tom tore up the sleeves of his hoodie with his pocketknife, handed them to Penelope and she went to cover the children's mouths, while he went to cover Daisy's.

They looked at each other in concern, unsure of what to do or what to say. Though a nice idea, the cloth over their loved one's mouths wasn't doing anything, so they just nodded and went to hug each other.

As Penelope reached out to Tom, he faded into the smoke, and suddenly he was being carried away by men in gas masks and black combat gear. Penelope began to attack the men, throwing the whole weight of her body onto them, causing them to stumble.

One punched her in the face as she kicked him in the back of the knee. She punched him square in the jaw when he fell. The other grabbed a riot stick and was about to hit her in the ribs when suddenly everything faded. Penelope stood there, terrified and confused.

What the hell was going on?

Suddenly, out of nowhere, Tom was hugging Penelope and she forgot all about what was happening. He wiped the blood from her lip and smiled at her concern.

He gave her a big, all-consuming hug and whispered in her ear, "Fix the cure. I believe in you, my love."

Before Tom could hug his kids, he was dragged away.

Penelope ran to her husband, but everything else around her faded and suddenly she was in a memory. It was a memory she had worked so hard to push aside.

She was ten years old. She was in her father's lab helping him with his newest breakthrough, when the lights flickered in the basement, alerting them that someone had broken in.

Her father signed to her, "Go hide in that locker and don't come out. Do as I say."

Penelope frightened, listened to her father and went into the locker. Peering through the small grooves in between the locker door, she saw her father's lab wrecked and him carried away by a strange man. She hadn't seen that man since that night, until today.

It was the same man, but with greying hair, who had her by the throat now, unable to move; the man she knew as the director.

"Did you really think you could escape us? That it would be that easy?" he hissed, gripping her throat tighter.

Penelope did her best to fight him, but she couldn't even feel her body. Everything was dulled, besides her throat that he gripped menacingly.

"Did you really think you could provide a cure and I would do nothing about it? I'm going to take what matters most to you and turn it against you. You have no idea who you are messing with. You will never win."

"Mom, wake up! Mom, you're okay!"

John was shaking his mom's shoulders as she was having another night terror. She was drenched in sweat and screaming out his father's name. He stepped in to do something after Lily had crawled into her closet, hands over her ears, shaking back and forth. He hated hearing it too, but he also hated doing something about it. He felt like he was intruding on his mother's most vulnerable state, and she always tried so hard to hide it from them.

"Mom, please, you're scaring Lily."

The young teenager tried his best to wake his mom softly, knowing she couldn't hear him — she never could. He shook her more violently which seemed to do the trick.

Penelope woke up in a panic, knife in her right hand pointed at John, still unaware of her surroundings John was frightened, but he didn't move, still bracing his mom's left arm as she fully awoke.

"Oh, honey. I'm so sorry. I didn't—" Penelope paused, sorrowful at seeing she was the cause of her son's expression of fear.

He shook his head in protest, as she sat up, put the knife down and gave him a hug.

"I know, Mom, I have nightmares about that night, too."

Penelope didn't say anything; she just hugged her son a little harder.

"Is Lily okay?" Penelope pressed, knowing she didn't handle it as well as John did.

"She will be," John said, not completely being honest.

Penelope understood that this was just kindness. "I'm sorry…" Penelope said softly.

John just stared at his mother, lovingly and understandably.

So much time had passed — four years to be precise — and though Penelope saw John as the young man that he was, she wouldn't ever stop wishing to protect him from these things, no matter how well he seemed to handle it. *He must get that from Tom,* she thought to herself as he came back with coffee.

This was a sign he'd been up for a while, since he had already made coffee.

It must have been a bad one, she thought with guilt.

This horrible nightmare that Penelope kept having was unfortunately not just a dream. Four years ago Meno had attacked Kairos and taken, at random, half of their population, including Tom. The people of Kairos, looking for someone to blame, blamed Penelope. Penelope didn't fight them on this. In fact, she used this distancing as a way to focus on what she knew truly mattered —taking Meno down and saving Tom.

She spent the next couple of years, after slinking out of her depression, on three things: becoming the best fighter she could; finding a cure with the help of Hubert, the horticulturists, and resident scientists, who, too, funnily enough, had been ostracized; and finally but most importantly, keeping her children safe which in her eyes was accomplished by completing the first two.

There was, however, one little detail Penelope couldn't get over; a thought that haunted her and caused these nightmares to occur often. *What exactly happened to Tom?*

Tom awoke, not in a lab and not surrounded by what he assumed would be scientists getting ready to test and help him meet his demise. Instead, he was sitting comfortably in a bright, white chair, a coffee cup was resting on the table in front of him. Steam poured from it, while a man sitting across the table from him sipped a similar cup of what he could only assume was more coffee.

Tom's vision was still adjusting to the fluorescent lights bouncing off the bright, white walls surrounding him in this box one might insultingly call a room, when suddenly he could see *very* clearly.

The man sitting in front of him was recognizable. His heart sank, his heartbeat quickened and his mouth went dry.

The older man, who was far more manicured than how he appeared in the photos hanging on his walls in Kairos, was someone he knew. To Tom though, this wasn't a good thing.

The man put his coffee down, sat back and hit a button on a little recording device in front of him. A soft, stern, female voice boomed through its small speaker. "Do you know sign language?"

Tom nodded.

The man smiled and then signed a response. "My daughter has taught you well. It's very nice to finally meet you."

*

Penelope was now making breakfast in the kitchen for John and Lily. She was drinking coffee, which was her only breakfast, until John handed her a banana as if to say, 'Eat something will you.' She took the banana and ate it, sitting down cross-legged at the table, while John and Lily ate bacon and eggs.

It was all very quiet like it usually was after a restless night like last night. Lily smiled at her mom and she smiled back. She felt guilt with every nightmare knowing that Lily was never the one to voice her problems. Tom was always better at getting it out of them.

Damn, that still hurts, she thought to herself, as she sipped her coffee and handed Daisy some bacon, who, in her older age, took it gleefully.

"Plans for today, you two?" Penelope asked like she always did, presenting a soft smile.

"School lessons," Lily said vaguely, with a nod in response from Penelope.

After swallowing his food, John replied, "I'm meeting up with Parker. We have a research project on native flora, plant life." For some reason, he was still looking down at his food and avoiding his mother's eyes.

Normally she would notice this, but she was exhausted from patrols and the Epistemic meeting —the group of those still fighting Meno — last night. She simply just nodded and voiced her lie of farming for the day, saying that she was also scheduled for night patrol so they would have to stay with Mia for the night. John and Lily just nodded in reply, as this wasn't that odd of an occurrence. Their mom usually did this after having a night terror, not wishing to sleep.

After they had finished eating, they all went off to their rooms to get ready for the day.

Lily and John went to their shared room, with Daisy following and laying in between their beds as they got ready.

Lily jumped on her bed and laid down, always being the one to procrastinate. Usually, John did the same but today he was quick to change, and he began stuffing papers, food, and supplies in his backpack. He put a knife in his back pocket, catching Lily's attention as she sat up on her bed adjacent to John's.

"Interesting 'supplies' for a research paper, John," she said, questioningly.

John, still grabbing things, responded to his persistent sister, "Parker and I overheard the meeting last night."

Lily was tossing a bright-red apple over her head, as she laid back on her bed again. "Overheard or rather, spied on?" she said with a smirk.

"Tell me again the difference?" John said in a snarky manner.

She chuckled. "And what, so you're going to join them?"

"No, Mom is going to try again," John said quickly, causing Lily to shoot up and stare at the back of his head as he rushed around.

"Wait, what? But… nothing has changed. They know moms face; the director knows her face… that's stupid," Lily said in a panic.

"I know. That's why I have to do something."

"Let me help." Lily said, more serious than she usually was.

John turned around to look her in the eye and said sternly, "No."

"Come on, he's my dad too, and Mom is going to get herself killed!" Lily said, a little louder than she intended.

"Lower your voice! Mom will hear you," John said in a panic, causing Daisy to stir and lift her head curiously.

"Sorry. But come on," Lily said in a whisper.

"Next time, I promise. It's just research right now. We aren't going to go into the city. Just... take a look," John replied.

Lily scoffed. John looked away from his sister as he packed a jacket into his backpack. He wasn't sure if that was a lie or the truth, at this point. He hoped he would be able to do more.

"What are you going to do, anyway?" she asked, curiously and dismissively.

"I have an idea."

"Well, that's a start. The next step would be to tell me this amazing plan so I can point out its many flaws, so you don't get yourself killed or captured," Lily said still miffed.

John rolled his eyes. He zipped up his backpack and began heading out their door after petting Daisy.

"I'll see you tonight, sis," John said patting her on the head, messing her hair in the process.

She punched his arm softly and then hugged him. "Remember those eyes if you decide to try and be the hero and get yourself killed," Lily said, pointing to Daisy who was staring at both of them happily. "You'll break her heart if you don't come back."

John chuckled as he went over to Daisy to give her a kiss on the head and pat on her backside, before he began heading out of the room.

"Here," Lily said, tossing him the apple she was holding. "Just in case."

John smiled and placed it in his backpack for later, saying, "Thanks."

"They know Mom's face, though, John. How can we get Dad back? They have tried so many times," Lily said, trying to reason with her kindhearted but misguided brother.

"Yes, but they don't know mine," John said with a look on his face that gave off the impression he was about to do something really stupid.

Lily shook her head in disapproval as he walked through their bedroom door.

John wasn't as sneaky as he thought he was, walking a little too confident like some teens did when they got away with skipping class. If John was honest, he didn't desire to go as much to class with it reminding him of his father. Yet, at the same time, he heard his father's voice in his head every time he conveniently had something better to do.

'It'll be hard to understand the world if you never try to learn.' Or in a more sarcastic mood, 'You can't call yourself a smartass without the knowledge; that just makes you an ass.'

John smiled, thinking fondly of his father. He was the reason he fought so hard for this retribution; why he spent most of his days in the gardens with Hubert, finding the right combination of strain to mix their own actual 'cure'.

So, I guess in some way I was learning; just more of an apprenticeship rather than a well-rounded diet of knowledge, John told himself, as if convincing his dad's voice in his head that this was just as good, when after all, it was *for him.*

He would get looks from the seniors in the barracks who he would nod a 'Good morning' to, and they'd shake their heads in a disapproving manner, knowing he should be in class. He wasn't quite sure why, but seeing them in such a huff made him smile, always being a little bit of a rebel. *I guess I get that from my mom.*

Not that she would approve of what he was doing at this moment. After their father had been taken, and half of Kairos for that matter, Penelope wished for John and Lily to not be involved. John understood that at the time he had been a child, but that was four years ago. He was not a child any more, and they needed any help they could get. Just as they were making headways, they'd find something had gone wrong: the formula mixed improperly, someone's location in the city being compromised — all their good spies were missing. It was enough to make one think there was somehow someone tampering with their mission, but ever since Don was exposed of his connection to Kairos and been taken to the city with the rest of them, they hadn't had any problem with the citizens moving forward in their pursuit to take Meno down. Not that that would have stopped his mom, anyway. Those first few couple of months — well, years really — were not a time where anyone wanted to mess with her.

Even with their numbers dwindling and less people volunteering to participate, the only time his mother had raised her voice was when John had insisted on helping. With tears in her eyes, she shouted at John, "I already lost your father; I can't lose either of you. I won't survive it."

John shut up after that and just hugged his mom as she cried on his shoulder. He promised himself then that he would do whatever it took to bring his father back, not just for him and his sister, but for his mother. He would do anything for his parents. He knew that his mother was not okay with the sacrifice if he didn't make it back, but he was. So he kept his pursuits hidden from his mother. She'd find out eventually, but John hoped that by then he would have fixed everything, and she wouldn't be *that* upset. Suffice to say, John was quite naive. Either way, he figured it was worth it.

He had almost made it to the outer garden pastures finishing his coffee along the way, when he felt a hard tap on his shoulder, making him spill what little coffee he had left.

John turned around and signed to his laughing friend Parker. "You did that on purpose."

Parker tilted his head and responded,. "Maybe."

John knocked his friend on the shoulder as they picked up the rest of their walk, moving past the gardens and looking around in every direction as if half expecting to run into others. They knew this wasn't likely. They usually went out on patrols at night, which was less dangerous.

"Any trouble?" John asked Parker.

Parker shook his head. "You got the clothes?" he signed in anticipation.

John looked around once more and then opened up his backpack to show two, matching grey T-shirts and jeans, with matching shoes and socks.

"Cool," Parker signed, smiling.

John chuckled. "Not the words I would use, but yes, 'cool'. You ready?"

"Yes, are you ready?" a stern and furious voice came from behind them.

"Oh, crap," John said, knowing that voice anywhere.

Parker looked over towards the direction that John was now looking, hoping that Penelope would be so upset with John that he could go unnoticed.

"Hey, Mom, what's up?" he tried to say in a nonchalant way.

"Really? What's up? That's the best you got?" she replied angrily. "What about you?" she signed, looking at Parker.

Parker looked at John for help, to which he signed to him, "Don't say anything."

This, of course, made his mom look at her son with a disappointed look and crossed arms. She walked over, staring at them furiously and with disappointment, the way only a mother could. She then grabbed her sons backpack to see what they were so excited to be looking at.

"I would have preferred it to by alcohol," she said, throwing the backpack back at John.

"Well, then, good news. I have some in my closet."

This made Parker laugh, until Penelope turned her gaze at him.

"You guys think this is funny? Do you think what happened to your father was funny?" Penelope said with more anger than she'd ever experienced before.

"Of course not! That's why we want to help, but you won't let us!" John said, very upset himself.

Parker was feeling very out of place now, looking anywhere but at them. He focused his attention on Daisy who wouldn't stop staring at him with those loving eyes.

He was interrupted by Penelope putting her hand on his shoulder to make eye contact. "Don't be mistaken by Daisy's kindness; we are both disappointed in you," she signed to Parker.

"Yes, Ma'am," Parker replied, looking back at Daisy and thinking to himself, *You still love me, don't you, Daisy? Of course, you do.* He was reassured at this when she licked his face, her tail wagging.

"You're weak, Daisy," Penelope said under her breathe not actually meaning it.

"Mom, we were just going to take a look, do some recon and—"

"You think it's that easy? You need to have name tags, identification, information and proper responses to the perimeter security, so you don't get caught. You need—"

"I know this — look," John interrupted, and pulled out two IDs and name tags for him and Parker.

Penelope was shocked. *These are actually pretty good,* she thought to herself, but she wasn't going to voice it.

"Where did you get these? And how did you know you'd need them?"

"Parker made them. He has a surprising knack for it. And no offense, Mom, but your meetings aren't that hidden."

Penelope rolled her eyes at John. "So, you've been spying on us."

"Well, you don't want us involved."

"Exactly, I don't. You should be in school."

"Aren't you the one who told us that we should be doing everything we can to help make sure everyone has access to education?"

"Yes, that's why I'm fighting for that. You're not helping anyone by sacrificing your education and well-being to bring education to them. Who's going to educate them if no one has gotten an education themselves?"

"Mom, you know I'm not going to be a professor," John joked, thinking that she was putting unrealistic expectations on him.

143

This only made her angrier, as he seemed to be missing the point entirely.

"Everyone is a professor in their own field. Find something you love and learn about it. Then show others how to do it to. That's education."

"Well, what if what I love is this," John retorted.

Penelope sighed to herself, as her own words were now being thrown back in her face. "It's too dangerous, John, and you're just a child. Besides, as good as these are, you still aren't educated enough in these measures to actually help. You need to be taught more."

"Then teach me!" John said in a raised voice.

He immediately regretted it when he saw the look on his mother's face. Penelope, however, let it slide, as she knew where his frustration was coming from and it wasn't intended for her.

"You shouldn't be worrying about these things just yet. You should be in class trying new things; becoming well-rounded. It's what your father would want. You're still a kid, John," Penelope said, concerned.

"Don't you think the children in the city, the families, deserve those same opportunities? I not only can help, but I want to! I'm learning what I need to, but this is more important than what they are teaching us. Half the information is outdated, anyway."

"Still, the answer is no."

John sighed as he furiously put his backpack back on his shoulder and started to walk off with Parker.

"But—" Penelope added with a sigh, as if she was going to regret her next words. "You can help. After your classes, of course."

As John went to interject, Penelope put a hand up to stop him. "You're not going into the city. I will allow you two to sit in on the meetings and contribute, okay?"

John and Parker looked at each other in excitement. "Thank you, Mom."

"And you will help Hubert in the lab, got it?" Penelope said sternly, and John nodded in agreement.

Penelope smiled at her son and Parker, hoping that this wasn't a terrible mistake and thinking that maybe she had been too harsh in the past. *I am kind of proud of him.*

"Now, let me see those ID's again," Penelope said, her hand outstretched, making John and Parker look at each other with a hopeful smile.

They were both thinking the same thing. *We are in.*

Chapter Nine

A young man around the age of eighteen could be seen bumbling through the town square moving passed vendors doing their business before they closed shop for the day. Everyone looked at him in horror as he was causing a ruckus in what was once a peaceful afternoon in Kairos.

"'Scuse me, oops, sorry!' he shouted, as he pushed through group after group of people.

No one thought his sentiment to be sufficient, but what he was late for was far more important to him for him to even care.

After a few minutes of sprinting at full speed he stopped, out of breath, at the entrance of Kairo's most established greenhouse. This had been proven to be very helpful during the winter months; a point that Hubert, the head horticulturist, who was short and hunched over in his old age, having spent his years far too often bent over in his gardens, was all to smug to demonstrate.

The first year that Hubert went about constructing it, everyone huffed and puffed about his numerous requests and not so kind 'suggestions'.. For instance, he would berate them on how they were building it wrong or how they were just a bunch of bumbling buffoons.

This, of course, was many years before Penelope and her family arrived, but when he told her the story, stating how he was never wrong, she just laughed, gave him a pat on the shoulder and asked, "And why has it taken this long for us to meet?"

Hubert shrugged, his cheeks blushing and his voice barely audible. "I'm a quiet person. I get along better with plants than the rest of these insufferable bastards here."

This really made Penelope laugh. "I can relate. They're not all bad, though."

After Tom's capture however Penelope felt more like Hubert, isolating herself from the community. That, of course, was besides with her children. They were getting to the age, though, where they had their own friends. Penelope did have a few confidants, mainly those who were part of the guard. No one could really fill that void that rested so kindly on her ever-waking conscience. Working helped, and so did Hubert's pessimism. There was something just so comforting about pessimism in situations like Penelope's, though she wouldn't ever admit why.

These past couple years it was uncertain whether Penelope and Hubert were close because of common sorrow or the same goal. They connected most once

Tom had been taken as she had become more bitter, and therefore, in the eyes of Hubert, was more like him.

"Sorry, I know I'm late," John said, as he opened the main greenhouse doors.

He found his mother, Pat and Hubert at the back of the greenhouse, looking very strainingly at a plant that Hubert was holding up in excitement, and there were looks of confusion at its significance on the rest of their faces.

None of them seemed too bothered by his tardiness, except his mother, but it was only slightly as he was probably late from school, and after many lectures in the past that ended with John reminding her that she was the one who told him he needed to go, Penelope stopped desiring to be reminded of that. A soft roll of the eyes sufficed for now, every time he showed up late.

"No worries, John. Come here; have a look. Maybe you can see something we can't. Hubert swears there's something special about this strain of the copious," Pat, said, scratching his head.

John chuckle softly, grabbing the SEM scope Pat was holding.

"The boy will get it; he always does," Hubert said proudly.

He had taken John under his wing years ago with John seeming to have a knack for herbology —that or a serious interest in it. Either way, to Hubert, that was a first.

John tried really hard to look for something, anything different, but he saw the same thing he saw yesterday, and the day before that, and the day before that. The cure wasn't working.

"Sorry, Hubert, I have to agree; I don't see a change."

"Don't listen to the boy, he's an idiot," Hubert said, moving them out of the way to look at it again himself. "How do you guys not see it! Why do I always have to be surrounded by idiots?" he asked, baffled.

They were all rolling their eyes at him, being used to him talking so lovingly to them.

"Must be hard being you," Penelope said sarcastically, but Hubert must not have gotten the joke, as he nodded in agreement.

"Just tell us, will you?" Penelope pressed, voicing what they were all thinking:

You're just going to tell us, anyway; let's just cut to the chase.

Hubert Sighed conceded, "Fine. Some of the filaments aren't as soft on the edges, meaning we are getting closer." He said with eyes that read he was excited or had finally gone insane.

"Are you sure you're not just going crazy? That seems more likely," Pat said, making Hubert angry and causing Penelope and John to laugh.

"Let me take another look," John interjected, as it looked as if Hubert was going to say something not too nice to Pat, if history proved anything.

John tried even harder to see it, now looking for exactly what Hubert said he saw, but it was difficult to tell. What Hubert was mentioning took either a real keen eye to notice or much better equipment to detect.

Before John could voice how he still didn't see it, Penelope spoke up. "Look, if you say it's there, I believe you. You are the one who got us this far, and if you think it's working, then it's worth a try."

"Thank you. Though I'd prefer if you all had better vision so I could hear you say I was right and mean it," he said begrudgingly.

"Me too," Penelope said, smiling at Pat who was rolling his eyes in response to Hubert's last glare.

Suffice to say, Penelope was the most used to Hubert's not so kind remarks.

"So, what does this mean, then?" Pat asked, handing Penelope and John a beer.

Hubert brushed off the offer. He was never one to partake unless on really hard times; for instance, when the last cure failed and they had lost a couple people in the city.

"We need more of the cure; we need more of their formula to test its effectiveness."

They all took big sips of their beer, and then Penelope sighed. "All right, I'll go."

This made John anxious, and the room went quiet. The last couple of times that Penelope had gone, it was close calls — *very* close calls.

Feeling the tension in the room, Penelope interjected, "Look, I'm the only one who worked at the lab. I know how to get in. Do any of you?"

"No, but you could tell us how," John spoke up, and the room went quiet, everyone was staring at Penelope and waiting for her to respond.

"John's right, Penelope. They are looking out for you now," Pat said, anxiously.

"I understand that, but I'll be careful. Besides, I'm the only one with a passing ID to get in the building."

John was about to interrupt, but his mother beat him to it. "And no, Parker isn't that good."

The room was quiet. No one liked this plan — it was too risky.

"When do you need it, Hubert?" Penelope asked, moving forward with the conversation, being the only one ready to.

"As soon as you can. This sample won't last long in these primitive conditions."

By primitive conditions he meant not the sterile lab he had run in the city over thirty years ago.

"Okay, I'll go tomorrow."

"At least let us go with you," Pat pressed.

Penelope looked at Pat and then her son. She didn't want to put either of them in harm's way, but she did agree it would help a lot.

"Fine, but you guys stay back and do as I say. And John, I really mean, do everything I say. Understand?"

Pat replied, "'O' course."

John followed suit, saying the same thing. Feeling a mix of emotions, he was finally allowed to go on one of the recon missions, and into the city, too. It was what he had been waiting patiently for. He was excited and terrified. *Just don't throw up until you're alone,* he thought to himself, feeling it rising in his throat. He told the others that he had to use the restroom, not sure any of them bought it, but then again, they were probably too anxious themselves to notice.

*

As much as John was excited to finally be going on a recon mission to the city, he was equally terrified. If he was completely honest, he never figured he'd actually be allowed to go. Even as an adult he imagined that his mom would stop him, as she was in charge of the ventures into the city. Yet today he was getting dressed to do exactly that.

It was eerily quiet in their little bungalow. Lily wasn't speaking to either of them after the yelling and shouting last night when she was informed that she would not be able to go with them.

Outraged by her mom and feeling betrayed by her brother, she was doing the one thing that hurt John and Penelope the most. She wasn't speaking to them at all.

John would never admit it, but it was excruciating to not have his sister to confide in, especially in such terrifying times, but he had to be strong. He had to do this for his dad and for his family. So he pretended to be okay and swallowed his emotions. The only remanence of his internal panic was the shaking of his hands when he was stuffing his bag with rations and emergency supplies.

Lily was watching him with concern, blanketed by a sour look on her face and crossed arms. Daisy came in and tried to comfort John by rubbing her face on his leg, but he was so wrapped up thinking about the fact they must really be in trouble if his mom was willing to take his help, that he didn't realize his thoughts had stopped him from moving his hands holding his backpack. He was just standing there, spacing out.

Daisy went up to Lily and curled up on her bed, giving her a wet, sloppy kiss to the cheek, causing her anger to reside slightly.

She looked at Daisy, and whether it was Lily's own voice in her head or what she thought Daisy was getting at, Lily rolled her eyes and spoke up, startling John from his 'meditation'.

"You will be fine," she said, in more of a condescending tone rather than the comforting one she had been planning on using.

"Huh?" John said, not really hearing her.

"Mom's not going to let you go far into the city. You'll be fine. You'll probably not even make it out of the woods. You'll be okay," Lily said, petting Daisy as a way to release her anger, so she could try and be comforting.

"Thanks. I really wish you were coming. I mean, I don't, because it's dangerous, but I'll miss you," John said, as he zipped up his backpack.

Lily smiled to herself, John's back still turned to her. She went and hugged him from behind, which he accepted gratefully as it was grounding him.

"I know you'll be fine, but come back, please. You guys are all I have."

As if Daisy could understand them, she brushed against Lily's leg, making her chuckle.

"Besides you, Daisy, of course," Lily said, crouching down to hug her as John reached down to pet Daisy, as well.

"We will," John said, as reassuringly as he could.

Then as if he was thinking something over, he went and reached into his bureau and pulled out an old leather-bound notebook. Lily gave him a confused look.

"This is dad's —his notes and theories. I was waiting until you got a bit older to show you. The stuff isn't cheery stuff; it's on Meno."

Lily's eyes perked up.

"Mom let me borrow it, now read up. We will be needing your help taking them down," John continued, smiling.

Lily smiled back, running her hands gingerly over the worn cover as if she could feel her dad's presence. "Thanks, brother."

"John, you ready?" Penelope shouted from the kitchen.

The three of them got up and headed to the kitchen, each with separate thoughts.

Here we go.

Time to say goodbye.

Treats?

One pat, two pat, one pat again, impatiently on the steering wheel, to a soundless rhythm in John's head. This continued for quite some time, driving Pat even more crazy than he already was being reduced to a babysitter. *If my naval officer saw me now,* he thought begrudgingly, but Penelope was persistent, and to be fair, she was more qualified for what pertained to this mission.

She knew the city better and was best at sneaking around for recon. She had proved this many times in Kairos: making him jump randomly with a cup of coffee, walking peacefully in the park, sleeping; all of which was accompanied with copious amounts of laughter from Penelope, with one final remark from Pat one morning, "You've proven your point! Leave me alone, woman!"

They were close, especially since both of their husbands had been taken by Meno many years ago. It was also why Pat was particularly disgruntled to be sitting on the sidelines, staring at the cemented city only feet away where his love was a prisoner, and where the men and women of Meno lived that he wished to kill. Yet he was supposed to just sit here.

His hands gripped tighter on the seat he was sitting in, with John continuously patting on the steering wheel. Both seeming to be dealing with this task differently.

"Would you quit it?" Pat said in frustration, causing John to stop abruptly and apologize.

Pat sighed, not meaning to come off so harsh. "I'm sorry. I hate this; just sitting here. The drumming wasn't helping."

"I understand. I hate this, too."

They both looked at each other in a consoling way, and Pat did what his name suggested he was born to do. He gave a fairly rough pat to Johns shoulder that John laughed at with a cough, thinking that it was probably meant to be comforting rather than painful, so he forced a smile.

"How do you think it's going?" John asked anxiously, trying not to show his concern.

Pat realized, in this moment, that as much as he was having a hard time, John was dealing with worse. His dad was captive and his mom was in the city right now, and there was a possibility of losing them both. So instead of being realistic, he decided to be uncharacteristically optimistic.

"Are you kidding? Your mom was born to do this. She will be back soon."

Pat wasn't as good at optimism as he thought, for John saw right through it. He had gotten to know him quite well over the years. This was Pat lying.

"If pretending to be optimistic is you trying to help me, please don't. It just makes me feel like there's something horrible you're trying to save me from."

"Understood," Pat said with assurance, looking at his watch. "My god, it's only been an hour."

John leaned back as best he could in his chair, preferring to fixate his attention on the sky with its many clouds above than on the cement city looming in the distance.

Pat took a different approach. He opened up his flask and decided to take the unhealthy route of staring angrily at the city, thinking of all the ways he'd get his revenge. *It'll be slow and glorious,* he thought gleefully to himself.

Penelope, on the other hand, was not having such a relaxing time, though the stress and anxiety was definitely the same. She appeared confident and strong, and it wasn't to say that she wasn't, but now that she was alone and actually in the city, she felt pressure and fear that she refused to acknowledge. She hated being in the city; from the lack of difference in any of the architecture to the uniform pillars and lamp posts that she imagined if measured, would all come out to the same exact dimensions. Not to mention, the muted color — grey. As an artist and a human, it gave her chills. But the thing that haunted her the most was how quiet and still it was. There were no tree branches to guide the soft breeze, no birds chirping, no hum from the Muni station.

There wasn't a single pigeon in sight which was quite terrifying, because it made one realize that nothing *lived* here.

Even the mechanics of progression where transportation was concerned was uncharacteristically muted. It made her feel exposed, like any small movement or expression she had grown so used to being able to express would give her away.

This fear was amplified by the fact that she was currently sitting on a busy Muni car, surrounded by citizens of Meno, all of which were on their morning commute to different sections of the city. Penelope sat there as relaxed as she could manage, trying her best to copy any mannerisms, or lack thereof, from those around her. She tried her best to remind herself to always smile and to not stare at others, no matter how intriguing they were with their muted movements. *My face is going to hurt after today,* she thought to herself, straightening her posture and her smile.

She knew they weren't paying attention to her. She knew that her outfit and demeanor would be sufficient, as she had done this many times before. She wore a grey-hued suit jacket and matching skirt, with a very itchy white button-up underneath. Her hair was tied up in a tight bun, making her head hurt. She knew that she fit in just fine, with her legs perfectly crossed and her terribly inconvenient black heels placed softly together. But every time she was here, she still found it hard to imagine that she seemed anything like these people.

As she reminded herself that she had been fine in the past and that she had nothing to worry about, she couldn't help but find her hands slightly shaking, which she quickly covered with her purse. This was the first time she was actually going into the building she used to work at. It was the most heavily guarded building in Meno — the medical building. The fogged-over memories she had kept swirling in her head until she forced herself to think of something else, as this was definitely not helping.

She decided to go over every single step she had to do when she got there, in hopes of calming her mind. All of this was made even more difficult by the fact that she had to act happy and content surrounded by zombies, on high alert for difference. The slightest movement out of character could cause someone to take notice and then everyone would. If history had proven anything, that would be very hard to shake, and her mission was too important to create potential hiccups like last time. Penelope had thought she was minding her own business when she turned a corner to find a resident talking to a peace officer, who was looking directly at her.

Looking back, she probably shouldn't have run — it could have been anything, even simple pleasantries. But she had panicked.

Can't do that today, she told herself sternly.

Penelope sat there in mindful repetitions, as a soft bell rung through the perfectly placed speakers on either side of her compartment. The doors opened. A soft, yet sharp female voice spoke over the intercom, sending shivers down Penelope's spine.

"Platform three."

One more stop.

She continued her repetitions, only getting sidetracked every now and again by the oddest of thoughts for people in her situation.

I would love some chicken wings right now.

Penelope had an unfortunate and inconvenient habit of getting hungry when she was nervous.

"Platform four," the crisp, annoyingly perfect voice boomed through once again, this time saying what Penelope was waiting for.

Penelope got up in the calmest manner she could muster, following two other employees, and began to follow their lead in a perfectly acceptable and normal distance. She followed them as they exited the Muni station and took a right under the Muni overpass. They walked across the street without looking both ways. At exactly fifteen feet away from the twenty-story medical building, Penelope pulled out her ID badge to show the peace officer outside the building, and she entered through the grand, double-paned glass doors, making sure to make a mental note of every movement and action for future reference.

So far so good, she thought, as she continued moving her way through the building. It shouldn't have come as a shock to Penelope, but the building, so far, was exactly how she remembered it. It was eerie to be back here. It felt... *revolting.*

The grand, polished, metal front desk was amplified by its sharp, cold features and a light-grey carpet leading to the desk. A young woman sat staring intently at the paperwork in front of her that Penelope doubted was as fascinating as they made her think it was.

To the left of the front desk was the stairs to the other floors, and even further to the left was an alcove of elevators where the rest of the employees were waiting patiently to get on.

Penelope made her way there, making note of the many security cameras around her as best she could, using only her peripherals.

In no time at all she was in the elevator, going up to the fifteenth floor. She grabbed a white lab coat that hung on a hook next to the lab entrance doors and attached her ID to the outside. She also grabbed a clipboard from the shelf next to it and began blending in, fitting into her old role, secretly looking around for the formula Hubert had specifically asked for —the strain of the cure he had been modifying in Kairos.

"Number four-two-five-six-seven-one," she repeated on loop, as she pretended to write things down on her clipboard, open sample drawers and check dilutions.

Hours passed with her moving from lab to lab, checking inventory and running periodic tests. She smiled at the employees around her when she entered the room, and then they went straight back to their work with no further interaction.

It was creepy, but Penelope couldn't deny right now that it was indeed helpful.

In laboratory four, Penelope found exactly what she was looking for. She acted like something wasn't right with this one and tossed the entire vile in the trash for Pat to come collect that evening, disguised as a custodian. With so many cameras on Penelope, they thought it best to not try and pocket it.

Penelope began to complete a normal workday as to not draw suspicion, which was proving to be a bit difficult. The longer she was there, the more chance there was of someone realizing she was in fact not doing anything at all. That being said, it was better than just leaving. No one left early, and if they did for any reason, it was because they were going to see their doctor.

A few hours later, and two hours away from Penelope being able to pretend to be done with her shift, she was in the filing room next to the elevators, perusing some clerical data she had found on someone's office desk in lab room six. She hoped that person wouldn't notice it was gone, as she had run out of other things to pretend to do.

Like every room in this building the walls were glass, so one could see everything and anything going on around them. So when Penelope heard the elevator doors ring periodically, she would softly look towards the elevator to make sure she wasn't compromised. Most of the time it was lab workers; sometimes it was peace officers doing their routinely patrols on the hour, every hour, but this time it was different, and she wasn't the only one noticing it. That was the thing about repetition — when it was enforced so highly, everyone was bound to notice a change.

Penelope was thankful to see everyone stop working and turn to see the commotion, so she was able to as well.

To her horror, she saw two peace officers guiding a shackled man to one of the exam rooms down the hall. Penelope's heart dropped as she recognized the man. It was Mike, Pat's husband. He was frail and spirit-broken. His blond hair was disheveled, and he was far thinner than she had ever seen him. She turned away, afraid he would recognize her and cause a scene, though his head was permanently fixated on the floor as they moved.

Her heart was pounding, and all reasoning for the plan she had went out the window. She couldn't calm down, so she set her folder down and walked in a normal manner down the hall in the other direction to the bathroom, as she began to throw up in her mouth.

When she made it to the bathroom, she took a quick and calm look around the bathroom to thankfully find it empty and without cameras. Like a veil that had been lifted, she rushed to the farthest stall and threw up.

If Mike's alive, then Tom could be, too; he could be here, she thought to herself.

Penelope refused to believe they weren't alive, but she also didn't know how to accept that they were after all this time.

She couldn't imagine what they'd gone through, and now seeing Mike that way... What had Tom gone through?

She felt herself on the verge of a panic attack, which over the years she had been able to maintain for the most part, but this was asking a lot for her mind to handle.

Just breathe, she told herself, as the room was spinning.

Penelope wasn't sure how long she was in that stall. By the time she had composed herself, she was thankful when she checked her watch to find that it had only been ten minutes.

With shaky hands she pulled herself up, straightened her suit and went to the sink for some water to drink and to splash on her face.

This changed everything. Penelope thought to herself.

Her heart told her to save Mike — he was right there — but their whole plan would then be compromised, and she would need proper clearance to enter the exam rooms.

What if I come back for him, with a proper plan set in place? What if I'm too late? What if he knows where Tom is?

Penelope didn't know what to do. She had never expected to see Mike. *What are they doing to him? What are they doing to Tom?*

Fear of being caught was quickly replaced by anger that Penelope had a hard time masking, as an employee entered the bathroom making Penelope quickly cover up her true reasons for being in this bathroom. She began washing her hands while the woman who entered went into the closest stall to the entrance.

For now, just stick to the plan, Penelope told herself, trying to remember why they were here and that it was the safest plan right now. But as she stepped out of the bathroom, she found herself moving past the labs, past the filing room, past the empty break room, moving directly towards the patient wing to find almost every room empty except one. The one with Mike in it.

The peace officers had left Mike alone on the exam bed, eyes closed and arms sprawled by his side, exhausted. The worst part to Penelope was that they didn't even bother to cuff him — they didn't seem to need to.

Seeing Mike this way made Penelope break inside. The funny, kind, musician that she considered a close friend, and the love of her best friend, Pat, who was just outside the city waiting for her to come back.

If he knew I saw Mike and did nothing... He wouldn't care about the plan.

Penelope went to open the door but already knew from experience that it was most likely locked. She had gone to test the handle when a peace officer called in her direction, making her heart stop.

"Hey, you, Miss,." the peace officer said, not taking too much care as to what she was doing like she figured he would.

"Sorry we were a minute. Had to go to the bathroom. Are you ready to begin the examination?" he asked Penelope.

Penelope was confused at first, until she realized that he must think she was the doctor for this patient.

"Not a problem. Let's begin, shall we?" Penelope ushered to the door, before her reasoning that agreed to sticking to the plan could catch up with the terrible idea she was coming up with. This was the last place for improvisation, and yet, here she was.

The peace officer paid no extra attention to her oddity and opened the door with his key card, ushering for Penelope to enter. She smiled and nodded a thank you as she entered the room, not quite sure what to do next, as the peace officers were apparently coming in, too. This was probably protocol — to help detain the patient should he have any energy to fight back. Mike didn't seem to be in any condition to do that, and the peace officers seemed to think so, too. One stood outside the exam room, and the other sat down in a chair in the corner of the room, staring at the adjacent blank wall of the exam room as if there was a movie playing there.

All of this was a very odd experience for Penelope. Being around people under the cure was one thing; having them interact like they were perfectly normal one minute and then robotic the next was just... creepy. Especially when those people had a gun strapped to their side.

Now that Penelope was in here, she didn't know what she was doing or how this was going to turn out okay. Any minute the real doctor was going to show up, and then what was she going to do? She hadn't prepared for this. She didn't know how to do an exam or what she was supposed to be doing, and now she had a peace officer watching her.

"Would you mind getting the personnel file for the patient, in the administrative room on level thirteen, for me? It hasn't been delivered yet, and I need it to begin my examination," Penelope said with a smile to the confused peace officer sitting next to her.

But he stood up and began to head out the door, sending in the other officer to fill his position. This one sat down in the same manner as the last, as if he wasn't a completely different person. Penelope took a risk and a minute later, asked for this officer to do the exact same thing as the last, having failed to come up with a different request. *It worked on the last robot; maybe it will work on this one, too, she thought.*

To her surprise he did exactly that, but just as he was about to leave the room, he turned to Penelope. "Are you sure you don't need my assistance with the patient?" he asked.

"Oh, no, thank you, he's a very calm patient," she said with a smile. *More like docile and barely alive.*

The officer looked at the patient who was asleep on the exam room table, nodded and left the room as well.

Penelope now had to work quickly. It would only take a few minutes for them to realize that there was in fact no personnel files missing for Mike, as they were on the tray next to her.

She turned to Mike, and quite aggressively, as she was in a hurry, shook him awake. "Mike, Mike, it's me, Penelope. Wake up."

As if expelling the only energy he had left, Mike opened his eyes as best he could. A tear fell down his cheek as if he recognized her, but he didn't have the strength to say anything. He just gripped her hand and stared into her eyes, with a soft grunt in place of speech.

"I'm here. It's okay. I'm going to get you out of here, I promise. We have to go now."

Mike could barely move, so she held him and ushered for him to sit up, but he was struggling to do even that. This was proving to be a lot harder than Penelope had hoped.

"Mike, do you know where Tom is? This is very important, please. Is Tom here, too? Is he alive?" Penelope asked in desperation, but Mike was too weak to speak or usher any recognition that he even heard what she said.

"Mike, where is Tom?" she asked once more, forcing him to look at her.

Suddenly security alarms went off throughout the building, alerting Penelope they were out of time and they had to get out of there now. It seemed that either she wasn't as sly as she thought, the officers had wised up or the cameras had seen her shaking a patient, which she assumed probably wasn't normal procedure.

"Crap, okay, Mike, this might hurt," Penelope said.

She forced him to stand up, and with all her strength, helped him walk out of the room.

When she opened the door, she saw every employee exit their rooms and stand in the hallway, confused and startled. They all looked at her, recognizing the irregularity of her actions of holding up a patient that should be in the exam room.

"Crap, crap," Penelope said again, as she quickly moved passed people with Mike barely keeping up, his arm over her shoulders and her arm around his waist, forcing him to move forward.

The only way out was the fire escape on the left side of the building. Lucky for her, that was just two rooms down. She ran with Mike in tow, blundering through the door, losing her heels in the process. They went down the fire escape as the alarm bells were silenced by the door being closed. It would take a couple of minutes before the city would turn on the rest of them, which meant they had a few minutes to get on the Muni before anyone noticed — or so Penelope hoped.

"She should be back soon; I wouldn't worry, kid. The fact that she hasn't made it back yet is a good sign. It means we are right on schedule," Pat said, as he watched John getting increasingly more stressed out and quiet as the day went on.

It was his first mission — it was always the most difficult.

John just nodded, as he didn't feel much like talking about it.

"I should go change. I'll be right back," Pat said, as he went to the back of the Bronco to pull out his backpack with the custodian uniform in it.

As Pat was in the back getting dressed, a distant alarm bell rang through the city causing John to shoot right up and yell for Pat, who had heard the noise, too.

"W-what is that? It doesn't sound good. Pat, what's going on!" John said in a panic.

Even Pat couldn't pretend to act like things were still fine. He zipped up his jumpsuit and closed the back of the Bronco with force.

"John, listen to me. Start the car, and I will be right back, okay? I'm going to go check it out."

"B-but—"

"John, stay here and start the car; I will be right back," Pat said.

He spoke with intensity and seriousness when looking into Johns eyes, as if to say, 'Listen to me and do as I say.'

John simply started the car with shaky hands, as he watched Pat run off in the direction of the city.

Several minutes went by, with the only sound being the rumble of the engine and the alarm in the distant. Pats footsteps had disappeared a long time ago and John sat there anxiously, listening for any sign of movement. He stopped himself multiple times from getting up to go after them, but he felt cemented to the seat, completely terrified. He tried not to think about having to go home and tell Lily that they had lost their mom, too.

Suddenly, footsteps were heard coming quickly towards them, and John saw his mom come running up to him. She gave him a hug, and John saw Pat right behind her, carrying his husband, Mike. His eyes filled with tears, but he was too shocked and relieved to acknowledge them.

"Oh my god. Mike! Mom, how did you—" John cried.

"Penelope, we have to go; get in the car," Pat said, putting Mike in the back seat and sitting next to him. He pulled the blanket from the back and covered Mike's shaking arms with it.

Penelope let go of John and got in the driver's seat. John climbed into the passenger seat, the shaking returning, as they blundered through the adjacent bushes and down the dirt road they had come from.

John thought to himself, *Does this mean the mission was successful?*

Chapter Ten

"You did what?" Hubert said furiously, when they got back to Kairos and told him how their plan hadn't quite gone according to, well, plan.

"I know, but what was I supposed to do?" Penelope asked, frustrated and upset.

Saving Mike had been the right call, but the cost of doing so was very high.

"You should have left him!" Hubert said angrily, not showing any sign of remorse for his words.

He meant what he said, and Penelope was a little shocked. She knew he was a grumpy, old man who didn't take kindly to others, but she thought she knew him better — that he was better than that. She was just thankful that Pat and John were in the medical building with Mike and unable to hear the horrible things Hubert was saying.

"Now, hang on," Penelope said, getting ready to show Hubert just how terrible that was to say.

Hubert put his hand up. "Uh-uh. You don't get to make me the bad guy here, or try and tell me how I'm a horrible person. You chose to save one at the expense of many; at the expense of your own husband," Hubert said with a raised tone.

Now he had gone too far. Penelope was furious, partly because of his horrible accusations involving her character, and most importantly, her husband. She also feared that he was in some way right.

"How dare you talk about my husband like that! You have no idea what I've been through and continue to go through. My husband is why I did it! Sure, maybe I shouldn't have taken that risk, but he would have wanted me to, and if Pat were in my position, I would have wanted him to do the same thing — to bring him back."

Hubert went to interject, to probably say something along the lines of how that didn't make it any better, but Penelope didn't give him the chance.

"I'm not finished!" she said, her voice booming through the atrium now, attracting the attention of passersby who had no clue yet what had happened.

"You don't know what it's like for us. I thought my husband was dead, and same with Mike. I thought that we had lost them both. You don't get to call me selfish or inconsiderate for this. I know what I've done, and I know what has been sacrificed, and I'm not proud of it. I will do everything in my power to fix this and save those innocent people."

She paused and sat down on the closest stool, feeling weak and exhausted.

"Tom could be alive," she continued, "This whole time in the city. I told myself and the kids he was, but I never imagined. Mike was barely alive. I thought he'd be given the cure, not—" Penelope couldn't bring herself to say it.

Hubert could tell that Penelope was already being hard enough on herself, as she sat down on one of the many stools around the big wooden table that stretched the length of the greenhouse. With her head in her hands, gripping her head tight, Hubert found himself in an awkward place. He had more to say — more to shout, really — but maybe a bit later.

He moved towards Penelope, but he didn't know what to do — he wasn't the comforting type.

He scratched his head to show how uncomfortable he was and then gave a rough pat on her back.

"You should go change; you look dreadful in that."

Penelope chuckled softly in between tears.

"I'll go start working on a new formula. They'll have changed it already," Hubert said, with a somewhat disgruntled tone but much less than how he really felt about how things had unfolded; which was insurmountable rage.

*

Months had passed in Kairos and not to be mistaken, in the city as well. Sleepless nights had occurred often, and new protocols had been put into place after approval

175

from an emergency meeting the first night they had gotten back from the city. Night watch increased and training and rationing had begun, in fear of another impending attack from Meno. Many residents fled. With the looming prospect of an attack on Kairos, they seemed to rather want to take the chance out there then stay here. Most in the community didn't blame them, and those who stayed wondered whether they should leave as well. Living in constant fear of their lives being ripped from them was not a place any of them were comfortable being in.

Suffice to say, they weren't expecting Meno to be too pleased with what they had done and what they had *tried* to do, and some residents grew angry and resentful towards those, in particular, who had caused such a disturbance. Harsh words were said and a few things were thrown out of aggression, and they took it because they knew it was warranted.

This led to big promises being made, especially from Penelope, who felt personally responsible for this result. These promises weren't without their reservations from the community.

Penelope had spent every day with Hubert and was even beginning to be okay with John and Lily joining in. Her views on their participation began to change after the last trip to the city, fearing that if something were to happen to her, Kairos wouldn't be prepared — her children wouldn't be prepared to fight back.

Hubert reminded her of something very important she had tabled. This was much bigger than her, and saving everyone insured that she saved Tom too. For this to ever work, it had to be about dismantling the entirety of Meno; it couldn't be a personal mission.

Hubert was still pissed off and made sure to let them know. He was particularly upset about the fact that Penelope would not be able to go back to the city, at least not in the capacity she had before. To John's surprise and horror, he was being groomed to now be the one to get the cure for Hubert when he perfected the formula, not that he was going to be able to get it the same way. That unfortunately, had been squashed. This, of course, was not something Penelope agreed with, but the training continued for now.

Pat, on the other hand, had stepped back. They were giving him some time to spend with Mike who was making a good recovery. That was besides his memory loss. After what he had been through and what they had probably subjected him to for testing, this was to be expected. He remembered his life before the city, and blurs in between, but most of his memories under the drug were a blur. This was Penelope's experience, too, in the past, which was comforting and not so comforting to Pat.

"Are you sure that Tom's alive?" Penelope pressed one night over dinner, making Mike and everyone else uncomfortable, as they plated more mashed potatoes on their plate and waited for Mike to respond.

"I think so," Mike said, not wanting to say one thing and it turned out it was the other, especially not on something so important.

"You think? You think, Mike?" Penelope said angrily, causing Pat to interject.

"Penelope, he doesn't know, okay?" Pat said, putting a soft, comforting hand on Mikes shoulder as he sat there, ashamed of not being useful. After all, she did save his life, and he couldn't help her.

"I'm sorry, Penelope, really. I wish I knew for sure," Mike said to Penelope, who forced a small smile and an apologetic nod.

Every day that passed caused Penelope to grow angrier and more resentful. She didn't regret saving Mike, but it didn't stop her mind from thinking intrusive thoughts. She would wake drenched in sweat in the middle of the night, unable to fall back asleep.

All those people could be free if you had stuck to the plan.

Tom could be home.

Tom is being tortured still because of you.

Tom is dead, now, because of you and what you've done.

The only thing that calmed the shouting in her head was exercise, so she would push herself and work out until it was an acceptable hour to go to Hubert's and do whatever she could to help.

On one particularly frustrating day for Hubert, with Penelope breathing down his neck and hoping for answers, he asked her kindly, "Piss off and let me work."

Penelope rolled her eyes and walked off fuming, thinking that she couldn't just do nothing. She was too sore to work on fitness training, so she decided to go by Pat's bungalow and check in. She wanted to see if he was ready for the next mission, as she was hoping to convince, or rather guilt-trip, him into going instead of John. In her eyes, he wasn't ready, and even if he was, she wasn't.

She waved to passersby who were scattered about throughout the short walk to Pat's. Birds were chirping and it was beautifully sunny out, with a soft breeze making it an otherwise perfect day for anyone but Penelope.

She approached his home, and right before she knocked, she heard laughter coming through the open windows, which should have made her smile. She hated herself for feeling the way she did in that moment, but the laughter, the beautiful weather, the cheery birds all made her angry, and that misplaced anger was about to hit Pat straight in the face.

Penelope knocked furiously on the door to which Pat went to open ten seconds later. To Penelope, in her current mood, this was far too long, and she stood there with her arms crossed and her face turned up into a furious rage.

Pat was understandably caught off-guard, and when he opened the door with a smile on his face to find

Penelope at the door looking upset, he quickly changed his demeanor, feeling the same way Penelope did.

How could he be so happy when Tom was being tortured in the city?

"H-hey, Penelope. What's up?" Pat said, trying to move past the awkwardness.

"I haven't seen you on patrols in a while, or at the meetings. I was worried about you and Mike, but clearly I shouldn't have bothered," Penelope said, with more frustration than she had intended.

If she was honest with herself, she'd be doing the same thing with Tom if she was in Pat's shoes, but she wasn't ready to admit that or think about those painful images.

Pat sighed and stepped out of his front door. He ushered Penelope to follow his lead as he sat in one of the two porch chairs outside his front door.

"I'm sorry, Penelope. I'll be there tomorrow, I promise."

Penelope's anger lessened slightly, feeling like a fool for thinking that Pat was going to just stop fighting simply because Mike was back.

"Oh, okay, well, great. We need to plan the next run. Hubert needs more strain of the cure; we were thinking next Wednesday would be good. I'd want to go sooner, but Hubert needs more time to pinpoint the exact one he needs."

"Okay, sounds like a plan, but wait, don't you think that's risky? Going back to the city, the medical building in particular?" Pat asked, concerned.

Penelope stopped making eye contact, as if the next words she was going to say were going to be particularly difficult to voice.

"That's the problem... I can't go. They'll recognize me. I was hoping you would. John's too young. I don't want him doing it; not to mention he wouldn't fit in and—" Penelope stopped mid-sentence, as she looked over at Pat's face filled with concern.

"I know it's a big ask with Mike back and everything, but we have to do it," Penelope pressed, making Pat angry.

"Why?" he said, without truly thinking of what he was saying.

"Huh?" Penelope said, giving Pat a chance to explain himself.

"Why do we have to do it?"

Penelope was in shock. "Because of my husband. Because of the innocent people in the city?"

Unfortunately, these reasons didn't seem to work the way Penelope had hoped they would, because Pat just sat there, staring off into the distance, to ashamed or embarrassed to look Penelope in the eyes.

"I know. And I'm a horrible person for saying this, I realize, but I can't risk losing what I have."

"You only have your husband back because of me, and you won't help me save mine? I risked everything to bring him back because I knew it was the right thing to do, and I would have hoped you would have done the same for me," Penelope said furiously, causing Mike to come out of the house to see what was going on.

Penelope knew she didn't do it just out of desire to have these actions reciprocated. Mike was a good friend of hers, and even if he wasn't, she didn't think she would have been able to walk away. But as selfish as it sounded, and even more, how it felt, all Penelope could think about since that day was Tom. She had to do whatever it took to get him back, and she felt helpless. She couldn't go to the city, and here her friend could solve this problem. He could help her. Whether it was fear or Pat had what he wanted to accomplish in the city, Penelope didn't know, but she was furious just the same.

"Penelope, I'm sorry. I just—"

"No, you don't get to apologize," Penelope said, getting ready to storm off.

"Oh, just admit it, Penelope. If Tom was here, you wouldn't fight; you wouldn't care!"

"Pat, that's enough!" Mike said, embarrassed, but the words were out there.

Penelope stopped in her tracks. Everyone in the neighborhood was now watching, including John, who was walking home with Parker, who happened to live right next to Pat and Mike's house.

Catching the end of the conversation John could tell that his mom was upset, and he went up to see what was going on, but Penelope was too fixated on her conversation to try and explain.

She instead moved past her son and walked towards Pat, who stood his ground with Mike trying to stop him.

"Of course I'd care! Are you kidding? This is bigger than me; than us. This is our entire civilization crumbling under displacency and imprisonment. This is my children's future; this is the future of humanity! I'm so disappointed in you! Tom would have been disappointed in you," Penelope said, moving closer to Pat who stood proud, not having anything else to say in response.

"I thought more of you, Pat. I thought you understood; I thought you were my friend. But above all else, I thought you were a good person. I guess I was wrong."

Penelope then turned around again and began walking off.

Pat shouted in her direction. "I'm sorry to disappoint you, Penelope, I really am. I'm sorry. I guess I'm scared. I guess I'm selfish. Call me what you want, but I have my husband back and I'm not going to risk any more of my life without him. Let someone else save them."

"Don't worry, I will," Penelope shouted back in anger, storming off into the distance.

John gave Pat a disappointed look and then turned towards the direction his mother went.

After Pat and Penelope had had an argument that the whole town could hear, word spread very quickly, and at the last town meeting, they promised to take a break from going into the city. You can only imagine how Penelope took this. She agreed, to save face, but as John already knew, she wasn't going to follow it. The thing that worried John the most was that she wasn't being careful anymore, and that was terrifying. Penelope was haunted; haunted by her own actions and even more so for what she didn't do. Every day that passed she felt the weight of her father, her brother and her husband.

Were all the men in my life doomed to perish? If Penelope was honest with herself, she would acknowledge that this could be why she was always so stern at keeping John out of this fight. Over the years, his desire to help proved to her that she needed to change. This wasn't something she could do on her own, and every day that passed they lost more members of the Epistemic.

Things needed to change; their tactics needed to change.

"All right, so you can't make the antidote last without the specific strain they are using, correct?" Penelope pressed, walking back and forth, hand to her mouth in deep thought.

She was in the garden with Hubert, John, Lily and what remained of the Epistemic; Mia, her son, Parker, Sherry and Bill. A few new members also joined them, friends of John and Lily's; Delilah, Sam and Ava.

Hubert rolled his eyes in a manner that suggested, 'Do we really have to go over this again?'

When Penelope stopped in her tracks and looked over at Hubert, awaiting a response, Hubert sighed and begrudgingly responded, "Yes, you know this; we all know this now. You've asked me that same question ten times in the last hour."

It wouldn't be far off to assume that Hubert was exaggerating, but when the collective looks on everyone's faces were clearly exhaustion, you could tell he wasn't lying.

Penelope, however, seemed to be ignoring everyone and just kept moving back in forth as if on a very short track, repeating this over softly under her breathe.

She stopped. "How long exactly does it last?" she asked, seeming to have a hamster running very quickly in her mind that no one else was picking up on.

"With my antidote as of right now, I can maybe guarantee the cure wearing off in a couple of years, but triggers of difference help."

A friend of Lily's raised her hand which made Penelope instantly like her. "What's a trigger?" Ava asked.

"A trigger is anything that sparks your curiosity. Here in Kairos, well, it's everything. In the city, it's quite hard to come by."

"Hence, this not being a proper solution," Hubert pressed further, as if this was solidifying a point.

"Of course, it's not the solution, but it's something," Penelope said, frustrated with Hubert's ability to shut down every suggestion.

Hubert was about to give a snarky remark when John interrupted.

"Question is, can we find a way to use this antidote to find the serum Hubert needs to destroy the cure?"

"I second that," Lily said quickly, bumping her older brother in the arm and making him smile.

Penelope smiled, too, because her son's words gave her a great idea.

"It's worth a shot, isn't it?"

Penelope wanted to go, but it was too soon after her last visit, and she hadn't necessarily gone unnoticed. Someone else had to go, and after months of debate, the one who ended up going was Bill, a handyman turned artist, over the years being taught by Penelope.

"You sure you want to go, Bill?" Penelope had softly asked the night before.

Bill smiled at Penelope and nodded. "They took my daughter. I'm positive. I'll be back before you know it."

"Promise?" Penelope said with a smile.

"Promise."

Every day for six months, members of the Epistemic went to the outskirts of Meno and waited for Bill to come back. Four months went by, and Sherry, the best nurse in Kairos, volunteered to go into the city, as well. Five more months passed and there was no sign of Bill. Sherry made it back after eight months in the city.

Bill was never seen again. People stopped volunteering after that, and no one expected them to.

They all agreed to stop, including Penelope. At least, that's what she begrudgingly said.

Chapter Eleven

Hiding behind a mossy tree on the outskirts of the safety barracks in Kairos, a young man in his early twenties with softened brown hair and even lighter eyes, was doing his best to not be noticed. He'd been there for what felt like hours, waiting patiently, anxiously and with an uneasy stomach, unable to eat the granola bar in his pack, worried he was right.

It was too early for patrols, and yet he heard footsteps; two sets of them, one softer than the other. He knew exactly who it was, and if he wasn't trying to stay quiet, he would have sighed out loud.

Mom, why do you keep doing this? he thought to himself in frustration.

A woman wearing dark-green utility pants, a matching T-shirt and combat boots, with her long, brown hair in a tight braid, came walking past eating an apple, with a Pitbull following in stride, carrying a dog harness pack on her back.

Neither of them seemed to be hiding their presence, which gave way to the obvious conclusion that, unlike the young man hiding behind a tree they were approaching, they were *allowed* to be there.

The boy was so fixated on staying hidden that he didn't notice when their footsteps stopped becoming prominent.

It took all of two seconds of him realizing this before he had a blade pressed to his throat by the woman he was following. Then came a big sigh of frustration from her and a lick to the hand from the dog.

"What the hell are you doing here, John? You're supposed to be working at the medical wing," Penelope said, tucking her knife away and crossing her arms in disapproval like any mom would in this situation.

"I knew you were going to the city. You lied to me and Lily. You promised after last time that we would stop; that we *all* would take a break," John said, quick to change the blame over.

"You're right, I did lie, and I'm sorry. I shouldn't have," Penelope said honestly, looking into her son's eyes with concern. "But I have to go. I have to fix this. I have to try; don't you understand that?"

"It's not that I don't want you to. I'm proud of you, Mom, for fighting so hard. And Lily and I want nothing more than for you to bring Dad back, but this isn't the way. I just don't want you to do it alone. I don't want to lose you, too," John said, with anger and sincerity.

"Everyone has given up after what happened with Bill. They don't want to fight Meno anymore. I don't blame them, but we can't stop. They can't win. There are more people going through what Mike did, and what

189

Bill is going through," Penelope said, trying to show John the big picture.

But John was still too afraid of it not going to plan, that he lashed out. "Dad wouldn't want you to risk our lives, the lives of this community and your life for him. You can't keep using yourself as a guinea pig. It doesn't work! Each time it takes you longer to get back. Let us help, please," John pleaded.

"You think the reason I'm fighting back is to do with your dad? Of course, I want him back, and I will continue to fight for him, but this is not about him. This is bigger than that. Your father was taken because of the fact that we were fighting Meno. This war started before then and will continue after. You may not remember what it was like to be in the city, and you were fortunate enough to not have to take the cure. But I remember. I know what it's like, and there are hundreds of thousands of people suffering," Penelope said angrily.

"But they don't know it, Mom!" John said, his frustration built up out of fear of losing his mom, too.

Penelope looked at her son with sadness in her heart at his words and then responded calmly, trying to remind herself that he was just scared, and he didn't know what he had said.

"I know you're afraid, honey, but just because people don't know they are suffering doesn't mean we should allow it to happen. *We* know they are suffering, and that is enough reason to try to fight for them. I know this is a lot I'm asking of you; to be selfless and to understand why I must go even if it means I might not come back. I don't want this to be your future —hiding away in fear of speaking out for injustices or expressing your difference. And as much as I don't want that to be your future, for those in the city, it's their present reality. Don't you think we should do something?" Penelope asked her son, who seemed to be infuriated by the fact that he did understand.

"What if there is nothing worth fighting for? What if it's too late?"

"Honey, there always is. I will never give up fighting for them and for your father, as he would for me. I love you, but I have to go now. I promise I'll be careful. Tell Hubert I'll be back in a couple of months," Penelope replied, giving her son a hug and Daisy a hug and a kiss as well. She then gave her son a look that read, 'Go back home now.'

She headed off towards the covered hole in the fence she used to exit Kairos in secret, while Daisy stayed by John's side. John stood watching, his hands placed firmly on the bark of the tree he had hidden behind moments ago. With his mother gone, he reached into his pocket, pulling out its contents. Resting in his now open palm was a small vile of blue liquid. It was a liquid that resembled the one that Penelope had carried with her into the city, a concoction Hubert had been working on for years. Captivated by its presence, he stared at it for a few moments before putting it back in his pocket, ushering for Daisy to go home. She obeyed, and John headed in the same direction his mother had gone, a little less confident than she had been.

*

Present day

John shot up, drenched in sweat, as his sister came blundering through with a tray of freshly brewed coffee, toast, and strawberry jam.

"Sorry, I meant to be quieter, but you'll learn very quickly that that isn't my strong suit."

"T-that's all right. Thank you for the breakfast," John said, catching his breath after waking up in a panic.

Lily put the tray in front of him, watching him suspiciously like everyone did after they were recovering from the cure.

"Interesting dream?" Lily pressed.

John tilted his head slightly as he took a sip of coffee. "Kind of felt more like a memory," he said, confused by his own words.

Lily nodded. "Yes, annoying, isn't it?" she said, with a look that said she knew exactly what that was like, as she poured them both coffee.

"I know it's good to get the memories back, but when I do, the whole process just pisses me off," she said with a soft laugh that John reciprocated. "I know, it's unreasonable. It just makes me feel like an idiot, not having my own memories."

John chuckled softly and took a sip of his coffee. "No, I get it," he replied, and if he was being honest, as odd as it sounded, he really did get it.

"Right, so, what was your dream about?" Lilly pressed, as she started drinking her coffee.

She was sitting on the edge of his bed, legs crossed comfortably, looking very intrigued.

John was in the middle of taking a sip of his coffee when she asked, so he shrugged his shoulders in an unsure fashion, then replied, "I think it was a memory of Mom sneaking off to the city. I was a bit younger, I think. It's a bit blurry, if I'm honest."

Lily nodded her head in understanding, handing him the toast after spreading a generous amount of jam on it.

"Yeah, she did that a lot. Understandable after everything that happened, but I hated those years. You did, too," Lily responded in reflection.

She took a bite of John's other piece of toast, as it didn't look like he was going to eat it. His attention was more fixated on the coffee in his hand.

Lily brushed the crumbs off her hands to pour more coffee into his now empty cup from the French press on the tray. "Well, we both felt helpless, really. Mom was hurting, dad was captured and Kairos was falling apart. We were kept out of it as much as Mom could maintain — that was until Kairos was attacked again," Lily said, pausing to take a sip of coffee like this wasn't a big deal. She continued, "Then they could use any help they

193

could get. Half of Kairos left willingly with the director when he offered jobs that would allow them to not be 'treated', and well, the rest who didn't wish to fight either fled or were taken eventually. Suffice to say, we grew up pretty quick, and damaged." She chuckled, trying to lighten the mood. "Sorry, hardened," she corrected.

"Why—I don't remember any of this, is that normal?" John asked, feeling sick.

With her mouth full, Lily nodded. "It happens when you've had the sickness so many times. Each time you come back a little less aware, one of the reasons I volunteer any chance I get. So that you guys can have a break."

"How many times have I gone to the city?" John asked, unsure he even wanted the answer.

Lily stared at the toast in her hands. "Too many to count. This time was the longest. You and Mom have been gone years. All I got in return was a lousy note; no offense. I guess you guys didn't want me trying to come with."

"Years?" John asked, confused, feeling even more sick to his stomach.

Lily pressed more bread into his mouth stating that it helped, though John didn't feel like he could stomach any more food; or information, for that matter. Years of his life had gone by, and he didn't remember any of it. So much of his past was foggy, and his head was killing him.

Lily moved his face towards hers as he closed his eyes, his hands pressed to his throbbing temple. With a mouth full of crumbs, she interrupted his much-needed silence.

"The only way out is through, eh?"

John nodded but chose to not agree.

"All the same, I guess it's a good thing I didn't come with you guys. If I'd known what it would lead to... No offense." Lily made a sound as if she got the shivers.

John thought to himself, *I'm not sure what part of this she thinks is helping.*

"Kairos fell apart pretty quick after you guys left. People felt there wasn't much reason left to fight. Well, some stuck around. The best of us," she said with a wink. "I've made my contributions too, see?" She rolled up her sleeve to show the black ink on her arm.

He had noticed it when he first met her, but he had then been distracted by the apple she had tossed him.

Black swirls on her skin created images of trees, flowers, a pigeon and something he figured was meant to resemble their dog, Daisy. And then hidden among all of these was a single sentence, one that now haunted him. 'Why are you happy?'

"Clever, right?" Lily said proudly.

"What is it?" John asked, as he was failing at identifying it.

"They are called tattoos. Or tittoos? I can't remember; Ava?" Lily said, yelling into the living room, with Ava responding as if they had gone over this many times in the past.

"It's called a tat-too. Think about it, my love; why would it be tit?"

"Why anything is pronounced the way its pronounced beats me," Lily responded. "Its permanent ink. I learned about it when we did a raid one year, in what seemed like an old art or creative school in the city. Completely abandoned. I doubt they figured it would be something they needed to destroy. We hit the jackpot there; my favorite raid.

"The point is that even if I get captured, I'll have something to connect to. Smart, right?" she said, as if she was particularly proud of this idea.

John kept looking at it, intrigued. "Yeah, unless they decide to just cut it off," he said nonchalantly, like his old personality heavily laced in pessimism was seeping through, as he took another sip of his coffee.

"Huh. Well, shit, that's a horrible image," Lily said, thinking this over and making herself laugh.

It wasn't until she laughed that John realized what he had said, not knowing why he had said that.

"Oh, I am so sorry. I don't know where that came from," he said mortified, by his own words.

This only made Lily laugh even harder. "I do. You're slowly coming back. I hated that, too. Again — genius," she said, pointing to her arm with a smile, seeming to choose to ignore the horrific plot hole in her idea that John had pointed out moments ago.

John smiled and realized he'd been snacking on the toast unknowingly this whole time, and it was in fact helping him feel better.

Lily poured herself some more coffee and cupped her mug in her hands, allowing it to warm her up a little bit before taking a sip. "Anyway, things will be different soon. Mom thinks she found a cure." Lily laughed to herself. "An actual cure."

"An actual cure?" John asked, as if saying it out loud would help it make sense.

"That's why she had me give you the signal. Again, my idea — genius, right? Plant the seed and the ideas will grow. Much easier and chaotic than what I've done in the past. Let's just say that throwing an apple into a crowd can cause one: a bruise and two: a lot of people in a panic wanting the apple. This was a lot more precise. Not that that was Mom's idea, either; you guys kind of left me to figure that one out."

She spoke of these events like they were as casual as workplace gossip next to the watercooler, though for her they could be just that. John, however, was still playing catch-up.

He thought over what Ava had told him the other day; some very sound advice. 'Try to just let things happen around you, otherwise you'll never catch up. Just nod your head for now.'

John did just that, while Lily looked at him as if to say, 'Are you mocking me, or have you been doing that a lot lately?'

"Anyway, I'll go over it later," she said, thinking over some advice that Ava had given *her*. 'Give him some time.'

Lily stood up, wiped her hands on her pants, finished her coffee and grabbed the now empty tray. "C'mon, get dressed and meet me out back. It's such a beautiful day out, and I'd hate for you to miss it. I imagine you don't remember many, anyhow. Not yet, at least," she said with a wink.

John laughed sarcastically, as if to say, 'Real funny', which made Lily laugh at her own joke.

He then nodded that he would meet her outside, and his sister left the room, allowing him the chance to shower and get dressed.

He couldn't remember, until this moment, that one could actually enjoy taking a shower. That is to mean, he'd never had a warm one or knew that such a joy existed. He may have let his mind wonder and his body settle too comfortably under the water for too long, because his overindulgence of the warm water was cut short.

Unfortunately, that joy only presented a frustration that he used to be so accustomed to when stripped from it. His eyes closed under the warm, running water that quickly and abruptly turned to cold, sending shock waves of emotion he now had the proper word for — annoyance.

He stepped back exclaiming his frustration.

In the distance, Ava shouted, "Sorry, John!"

John decided to get out of the shower as the cleansing process had ended several minutes ago; he was simply just enjoying the heat. Now that it had seized, there was no more reason to waste time.

He jumped as he looked at himself in the mirror for the first time, after recognizing what a mirror was in the first place, a very odd and surreal experience. Probably the most shocking part was the color of his eyes — a vibrant, bright blue. To have such vibrance right on his face and not know it. *How did I live not even questioning what I looked like? Or the fact that I'm much older than I thought...*

Now you're getting ahead of yourself, he thought, as if trying to reassure himself the best he could.

It was a weird feeling, when he got out of the shower, to pull out the drawers in the dresser and find so many pigmentations of color other than grey, It looked particular odd with the clothes he had been wearing, which were laying on his bed now, looking muted and lacking.

Torn by familiarity and comfortability and not knowing which they were connected to, he finally decided to pick a dark-green T-shirt and jeans, concluding that they were clean and they were probably more comfortable, which was confirmed after putting them on. He shouldn't have been surprised when they fit him so well; they were much more fitted and tighter than his grey suit.

I guess clothes being itchy isn't normal.

"Hey, John, grab a jacket. I want to show you something, and it's a bit cold out today! We have actual weather here, unlike the city," Lily said, with a snicker to herself.

John shook his head, chuckled and grabbed the hoodie on the back of the bedroom door.

He went to see how he looked in the mirror in the corner of his room, something that was already becoming a normal part of getting ready. He not only felt like a different person, but he also looked it. He put his hands in his pockets in a relaxed and unusual manner and found a piece of paper and a vile which contained a blue liquid in it, shining brightly when he held it up to the light to get a better look at it.

He was about to ask Lily what this was, when he saw the note had his name on it.

It read:

John, take this.
Love Mom.

Looking confused, John opened up the bedroom door to find his sister in the kitchen eating some cereal, feet up on the table and cat in her lap.

"Hey, Lily, what's this?" he asked, holding the vile in his hand.

Lily sat up. The second she saw what he was holding, she smiled.

*

Four years Ago

The breeze was pleasant and calming, but not as pleasant as the crisp, golden ale that Penelope was indulging in, while watching the setting sun softly warm and brighten the back garden of their weathered bungalow.

"All right, you were saying?" John said, coming through the back door that led to the deck that Penelope was sitting on the steps of.

Now back with a fresh, new pint, he sat down beside his mother, taking a sip and waiting for her to pick up their conversation.

"If you are on board with this, honey, which you know—"

"Mom, stop, we've been over this," John said, interrupting his mother.

Penelope sighed and continued talking. "Okay, fine. I've thought long and hard about this, and I've come to the only viable conclusion. I don't like it, and frankly, I'm reluctant. We have barely any people left of the Epistemic, they are all so young and I don't want to keep sending people into the city it's just not working." Penelope paused, looking at her son who had become such a wonderful man, thinking how horrible of a thought it was to forget him.

She didn't realize she was staring until John spoke up. "Mom, what is it? Tell me."

"It requires us going into the city." She paused.

"Yeah, what's new? We do that all the time," John said nonchalantly, taking another sip of his beer as his mom had lost the desire to drink hers since this conversation had started.

"This time without our cure, without a way back. We have to become residents. For this to truly work, to save them and to save your father, we have to take it down from the inside."

"But how will we be able to do that without a cure? Also, won't they recognize you." John pressed, confused.

"I've instructed Hubert to give us each the cure in a year. But if it seems to not be enough time, he is instructed to wait."

John's mouth got dry, and he gulped more beer as his mother spoke.

"As for me, well, I'll make some appearance changes to better blend in I guess." Penelope said this with detest.

"But that means we might never come back... there's no guarantee, is there?" John said trying to understand.

Penelope was quite for a moment, which answered John's question.

"Let me do this alone, all I wanted for you was to never experience that imprisonment, sure you've experienced it briefly but not without a way out, its…terrifying, trust me. I can't ask you do to this."

Penelope sat her beer down, desiring to hold her hands together in an anxious manner.

John wasn't sure what to say, he didn't exactly want to do this either, but he knew his mother was right. She wouldn't have come to John unless it was the only option left. If she was discovered than there would be no back-up. So, he paused and did his best to think positively though he felt quite uncertain that this would yield different results from the past.

"This will work. Besides, remember what you always say? We have to try, right? We need to do this; take Meno down once and for all. I'm in."

Penelope's eyes began to water as she looked at the man she raised — strong, and most of all, kind. The most painful and beautiful part, though, was that he had become the man she and Tom had always dreamed of, and he wasn't here to see it. All she wanted to do was protect him and Lily from losing those qualities and yet they are what drove him to help.

This is not going to be easy, she thought.

"I am very proud of you, my love. Your father would be, too."

This made John chuckle nervously and blush, moving away with a smile. His mother laughed and hugged him, which he was reluctant to reciprocate at first, but he finally accepted as they sat there together finishing their pints.

"What should we tell Lily? She'll want to help," John pressed, concerned.

Lily was conveniently out with Ava, her new girlfriend, unable to hear what they were conspiring to do.

"She will, trust me. We need all the help we can get. Unfortunately, she's made an 'impression' in the city that makes her a bad candidate for this mission. Besides, she'd hate it. Not that we will particularly enjoy it ourselves."

"Yeah, subtlety was never really her style, was it? Neither is conformity, for that matter," John said, laughing.

"Ah, mine neither," Penelope said with a wink, making them both laugh, with the setting sun softly leaving their smiling faces.

"This will work," Penelope pressed softly, with John nodding in reply.

This had to... she thought to herself.

Chapter Twelve

Present Day

The elevator ring was haunting. It alerted Jean that this was really happening. She had spaced out over the many floors in between what was a normal sector for her, to dizzying and frightening new floors where only the director and a small few were permitted to witness. Charlie even seemed a little queasy. That being said, next to Jean one wouldn't notice Charlie's small 'imperfections' of resilience.

The doors began to open, and though she knew it did not help matters, Jean held her breathe as if somehow it would stabilize her quaking legs and the sweat beading on her exposed forehead. Most elevators opened up to a hallway of sorts, but not at this level. No, it was just one big room. There were no separated stuffy offices cramped with employees, or a moment to compose yourself before interaction. She imagined, from what she had heard of the director, that this bucket of cold water of an entrance was exactly what she should have expected. None the less, it was not welcoming.

The room was bare like most offices, but with subtle personality, and surprisingly, not so subtle pops of color here and there, something that, for most citizens, was forbidden.

One could easily be distracted by this if it were not for the massive windows that had replaced the regular walls, overlooking the entire city — a view that Jean had never imagined witnessing. She always thought she would like the view, seeing the city from such great heights, but if she was honest, it actually just gave her chills. It brought up that voice in her head she was instilled to silence, the one that made her question, *Why is the director treated so differently?*

Why did he enjoy this view of overlooking the dark-grey, smog-covered city that below was filled with so many people, too little from this height, to be able to fully acknowledge them?

Maybe that is why. She thought to herself.

He was like a child looking meticulously at the ant farm he maintained, questioning why the ants were not happy and why they weren't thriving under his hand, convincing himself that the ants, in fact, were ungrateful.

Why am I thinking this way? The director is good, yet you are afraid of him, she tried to remind herself, unsure why.

Jean moved forward, following Charlie's movements, as their heels boomed through the otherwise silent office, while the director remained facing the skyline.

The chair was far too high to see what this mysterious person looked like.

When they approached the two designated red plush chairs in front of his sleek glass desk, Jean felt weird sitting in such an exuberant seat, as it was ingrained in them not to. She almost wondered whether this was a test, a test she could not risk failing.

Can they see me sweating? she thought nervously to herself.

But when Charlie sat down she followed suit quickly, as the director turned around.

He looked just like they did; no flair to his clothes and no exaggerated features. He was a bald, older gentleman with pale features and a terrifyingly genuine smile on his face, and what was worse was that it was directed at Jean, and Jean alone.

"Would you like something to drink, you two?" he asked sweetly, like a snake hissing before it strikes.

Charlie spoke up softly. "N-no, thank you."

The fact that Charlie was nervous made Jean even more nervous. *This was not good.*

"No? Coffee? Tea? Something stronger? I won't judge; I myself could use a top-up," the director said, shaking his highball glass that had reminisce of some melted ice and a whiff of something stronger.

Charlie shook her head, with a fake smile, and Jean, with the attention back on her did the same, adding, "No thank you," with a fake smile of her own.

He tilted his head in understanding. He then set his glass down, sitting back in his chair far too comfortably, as if he enjoyed the power he held over them, noticing very clearly that they were intimidated, and for good reason, if the rumors were true. They all knew there was a very short thread between them and the 'regular citizens' below, and it started and ended with that elevator.

"Do you know why we are here and they are down there?" the director asked coolly.

Jean didn't like his implication; as if the people in the city were vermin and they were treated this way for a reason, for the betterment of society.

No one responded to the director, but that seemed to be what he wanted, anyway. He seemed like the type that liked the sound of his own voice and would ask a question simply because he 'knew' the answer. He wished to use those he happened to be around as a sounding board to reflect his own values; who were all too afraid to speak against his 'opinions'.

Ah, the beauty of power corrupted, absolutely... Stop thinking this way! Jean battled with her unusual thoughts, unsure where they were coming from and why they were occurring when she needed to seem the most civil.

"Because we know better," the director continued. "We understand that what someone wants and what is good for them is not the same thing."

He paused to see if they were listening; of course, they were.

"This life is not meant for everyone. It's *hard* — torturing, even, to most. You don't know —you weren't there, and you didn't see the horrors it inflicted. No matter our advances through technology, ecology and social change, nothing was ever enough. Our species couldn't handle the fact that we were the problem, that we were the cause of all of these issues. We were, for lack of a better word, the problem we could not solve.

"So we had a choice: choose to destroy our species or, more realistically, make it so we can't see the problem. Do you see the difficulty in our decision? Why it was done and how we had no other choice? This is important, Jean. If you don't understand why, then you can't implement the solution."

Charlie tried to look at Jean to voice through her posture that she should answer simply and with the words he wanted to hear, but Jean was fixated in the director's direction, staring into his arrogant eyes. She found herself overwhelmed with a different emotion than compliance. Terrifyingly, she was feeling skeptical, and worse, in the eyes of her company, she was feeling curious. She reached into her pocket and gripped a crumpled up piece of paper, as if it had some silly way of dictating her emotions. She shook her head as a way of trying to fix the uncertainty she felt towards someone she was supposed to trust and believe in.

She still didn't even know why she was here, being told about the inner workings of their society, and from the director, of all people. They didn't once mention the employee she had evaluated, the whole reason they were here. In fact, he seemed calm compared to how this situation was treated at her weekly staff meeting just minutes ago.

They were both still waiting for her to respond. And she realized this wasn't about the person she interviewed, this was about *her*.

But why?

She looked to Charlie for answers, but her face was just as stoic and cold as it normally was. Her head was throbbing, and her palms were now noticeably sweaty. Everything she focused her attention on, trying to calm her headache, made it worse. Her mind was trying to cram all the new information into her head, about the items that enclosed around her that she had not noticed before.

"Do you understand, Jean?" the director asked in a harsh tone, as if he took her silence to mean she was not listening to him, which no one in their right mind had the nerve to do for his fuse was already only a millimeter long.

"I- I don't," Jean said honestly, her headache growing every second she sat there.

"You don't? And here I thought you were smarter than that, Jean."

Jean was no longer listening, or rather she did not seem to care, the pain she was experiencing being her utmost concern.

Seeming to have grown bored by this conversation, the director sat back and finished his drink.

"None of this is right…" Jean voiced, confused and frightened.

"What are you bumbling on about?" the director asked, not paying full attention to her words.

He then called in his assistant, using a button on the underside of his desk, as he seemed to be incapable of pouring himself another drink that sat inches away from him.

"This isn't right; none of this," Jean pressed, unsure of her own words.

Then, as if it was of little concern to the director, he said the one sentence Jean was terrified of. "Charlie, I think Jean needs to be taken to their physician. She doesn't seem well."

The director spoke as if he had finally ended their conversation on a good note, for there was no other explanation as to why Jean was not agreeing with him, other than the fact that she was sick.

"Wait, no, please. I'm okay; just a little headache, is all. Really," Jean pleaded, as a final ploy for self-preservation.

What's wrong with me? Why did I say the things I did? Why didn't I just agree to the directors wishes? she thought.

But nobody said anything. It was painfully quiet, and the director seemed done talking with Charlie, who remained a silent bystander. She might as well have been a fern in the corner, desperate for water.

Jean felt queasy. She felt like the sweat that was beading on her forehead was standing out like a bright, shining spotlight, showing how weak and vulnerable she was. And she could do nothing.

She looked to Charlie, who was staring at her shoes as if mentally removing herself from the situation.

The director's assistant came up and poured some more of the amber liquid, as he held his glass up impatiently.

"I think we are done here. Charlie? Escort Ms Jean out of here, please. That will be all."

Charlie straightened her posture and stood like a statue, waiting for Jean to come to her.

Jean's thoughts raced, wondering whether she should plead — beg — for her life, but it was clear no one here had a voice. They had no real choice, and she was no different from the citizens. The fact that she was on this side of the collective that turned people into slaves, was because she was so afraid of becoming one.

What have I convinced myself of? Her voice was quickly fading with every second she wasted sitting here. Before she was escorted to the doctor, she felt a rush to finally speak her mind.

"I'd rather be given the disease then be a part of those forcing it onto our citizens. I would rather lose my voice than take it from others any longer. It sickens me what I have been a part of. I may not have the strength to destroy you and this horrible place you call a society, but I will be happy one day to shake the hand of the person who does," Jean said, with such anger that her hands had turned white from gripping the seat she was sitting in.

The director laughed in his chair, as he began sipping his drink once more. He began smiling at Jean, throwing her off. Charlie, quickly catching on, stood there silently, doing her best to not be on anyone's side but rather a decoration fixated to the room, that had been mistaken as another human being.

Jean just stared at the assistant, who continued to smile at her like a proud mother. The director, still laughing, began to stop his cackle as he watched Jean.

He looked over at his assistant. His ego made her hard to place, but he did in fact recognize her, but from where?

"What? What are you looking at? Leave me," the director ushered to his assistant, and he sat back in his chair.

The assistant went to sit in the other chair next to Jean, ignoring his words, at which the director laughed, less confidently.

"And what do you think you're doing? Do you want to be sent to the doctor, too? You stupid woman."

He was trying to strike fear in his assistant, but she just sat there, smiling at him, with nothing else to say. It felt like hours had passed while she just stared at him, as if there was this big cosmic joke no one else was picking up on.

"What! What are you smiling at!" the director said angrily, slamming his glass on the desk, spilling amber liquid everywhere and making everyone jump, except for his assistant.

"Do you have any idea how long I have waited for this moment? I always imagined it being more… satisfying. Eh, well, when it kicks in, it will be."

Again, everyone sat or stood there, even more confused. The woman got up and went to stand next to the big windows that plagued every inch of his office. Arms crossed and in a firm stance, she began looking out the big windows, her happiness quickly becoming anger.

"You know, you claim to be so different from the citizens you enslave and feed compliance and conformity to in their never-ending troth. Yet, you are just the same. Look at you, with all your exuberance. You think you're somehow special? You're the only one who's allowed to be human?"

The Director didn't say anything. No matter how much he tried to speak, his voice was gone.

"First stage of his dose," the woman said looking at Jean, then she turned her attention to the director once again. "What gives you the audacity to take that away from people?" She was inches from his face. She sighed as she went to hit him and then stepped away.

He sat there seeming to be unable to move, as if his bodily functions were going out one by one.

"I thought long and hard about what I'd like to do, and most of the time it led to me killing you. But the more time that passed and the wiser I got, the more I realized that's an easy way out."

She went and grabbed the keycard inside the breast pocket of his jacket. "Thanks," she said sarcastically, as she shoved it in her pants pocket.

She then began to rifle through his other pockets, seeming to eventually find what she was looking for. She pulled out a bronze key from his left pant pocket and then used it open up the bottom drawer of his desk. She grabbed files and a smooth, glass flask that had a bright-green liquid in it.

The director looked at her, terrified.

Jean was even more curious about what she had grabbed. The only thing she could read off the top of the files was a single name in large font, scratched on a Post-it note: 'Mr. Parley.'

"Oh, don't worry, you're not going to die. At least, I don't think so. It's a horrible feeling, though, isn't it, to have no control at all," the woman said nonchalantly, not really seeming to care now, while staring at the view of Meno with a look of repulsion.

"Man, I can't wait to get out of here, and out of these clothes, for that matter," she said in disgust, as Jean unconsciously touched her own jacket, for it was basically the same outfit.

The woman then turned towards the director once more. "I wouldn't worry too much, just as long as you trust your subordinates. I just gave you a new form of the cure your scientists are working so hard on. I mean, really, you should try the product you force on to people. That's just being a good leader," she said with a smile, and patted him on the shoulder before she went to sit down, seeming to have collected what she needed. "Let me explain, because I think I'm getting ahead of myself." She was now sitting back in her chair, placing her feet up on his otherwise pristine desk. "My name is Penelope."

The director didn't flinch, as this name seemed to not mean anything to him.

"No? My father was Doctor Yarrow. You killed him twenty years ago. You also captured my brother and my husband — not that you'd remember any of them, I imagine. No, to you I'm probably nobody. I kind of love the fact that I'm the one to bring you down, as you have no idea who I am."

Jean sat there, her head ringing, trying to play catch-up and trying not to throw up. *Why does that name sound familiar?*

"Kismet, don't you think?" Penelope chuckled, now talking to Jean sitting next to her who was completely terrified and not fully keeping up anymore, though not from a lack of trying.

The director couldn't respond to this with anything other than his eyes and the look they provided. He looked like he knew exactly who she was, and in fact, he seemed pissed to see her, but Penelope didn't quite recognize this response. She was too fixated on her revenge, that it went unnoticed.

"I do, however, wish to thank you two," Penelope said, now looking back at Charlie who looked like she was about to faint, and then turning to Jean with a smile and wink.

"I—" Jean tried to speak.

Penelope reached over and put her hand on Jeans, as if to quieten her.

"Your protocol that is being enforced — I wouldn't have been able to help every citizen so efficiently without it," she continued, looking at the director. "Let's just say that the citizens of this city will finally have 'the cure', and you will be the only one to have the treatment you think so highly of... if, of course, you trust your scientists not to have made a mistake and kill you. In that case, you'll be too dead to be able to care." She laughed manically. "You have been pushing them very hard lately and mistakes are bound to happen. I do believe that luck happens sometimes," she said, gleefully.

Then, as if finding herself done with the director, Penelope turned to Jean and spoke to her softly, as if afraid of frightening her. "Would you like to come with me? I could use your help," she said.

Jean was hesitant, but she felt herself nodding, all the same.

They got up and Charlie moved to the side.

Penelope looked back, saying, "Funny thing is; that particular cure I gave you, I don't think that had a solution to reverse it yet. What a shame."

Penelope smiled as she got on the elevator with Jean. The last thing they saw as the elevator doors closed was the look of pure horror on the director's face.

Penelope began pressing the elevator button, more furiously than Charlie had but with different intention. Jean held her hand up to her forehead in some hope that it would aid her massive headache. It was eerily silent for a moment before Jean spoke up.

"W-what now?"

"Now, we go save my husband," Penelope said with anticipation, as the hum of the elevator caused a booming silence through the tiny tin they were standing in.

Jean gulped with the little moisture she had left in her throat and forced herself to respond. "W-what can I do?"

"We have all of Meno to save; I can use all the hands I can get."

She wore a smile so broad it felt like Christmas morning, though Jean didn't get the memo.

"It's going to hurt for a while. Just give it some time," Penelope said in a comforting manner, watching the numbers on the elevator go down. This, of course, only confused Jean further.

"W-what are you talking about?"

"The antidote; it's in your system. I put it in the office water coolers this morning. Did you honestly think you were free from 'the cure' too?"

Jean was still rubbing her head, having a hard time processing what Penelope had just told her.

"Wait, what?" Jean asked, but Penelope seemed to not be the best person to ask to repeat herself.

"So, you're a satisfaction representative at the Jameson production Mil? How's that been?" Penelope asked anxiously, as she watched the numbers above the elevator doors go down all the way to the basement.

Thankfully she had the director's keycard, as it was proven to be the only one that worked for that level.

"Oh, I was just filling in. I'm normally in a different division."

Penelope looked over at her, intrigued and confused. "Oh?"

"Yeah, it's called Kairos."

Penelope stopped caring about her mission for just a brief moment, fixating all of her attention on Jean and making her feel very uncomfortable.

The elevator doors opened, and a loud haunting ding followed as it opened up to rows and rows of dark cemented cells with lights flickering throughout the otherwise pitch-black hallway.

If she had thought that the director's office seemed out of place, this was much worse. Jean wondered whether it had been a smart idea to go with this woman, like she had previously thought. *Good job Jean, you always get yourself into terrible situations. Do you not have any self-preservation?*

As if flipping a switch, Penelope shook her head and stepped out of the elevator, not feeling quite as horrified by her surroundings as Jean was.

"Come on, let's go," Penelope told her. "We don't want to get stuck down here."

This made Jean's cemented feet pick up fairly quick.

Chapter Thirteen

Tom wondered whether he would ever be able to escape. Would he ever be able to change the mistakes he had made in the past that led him here to the city, away from his wife and children? As he sat in his empty, grey-hued room which was removed of any character, he placed his head in his hands in reflection. He asked himself whether they had finally gone too far. Would he ever escape this? Could anyone?

He chuckled to himself as he thought of how Penelope would react to his concerns. She would think they must be doing something right for them to take the care to be concerned.

This, of course, didn't change his situation in the slightest. He longed for, more than anything, above the push for change, above the ability to read literature again and to think contemplatively, above everything, he simply wished to have Penelope in his arms again, to hold John and Lily as long as he could and to feel the wet, slobbery kiss of Daisy on his face — to be *home*.

But this… this was not by any means home. This was emptiness. It was a world pretending to be blanketed in infrastructure —empty and devoid of anything of meaning. That's what he truly hated about the city. Like the taste of copper in your mouth before you threw up, there was always that terrible taste in his mouth in the city, even without the cure in his system —always on the verge of repulsion and perpetually on the edge of vomiting.

He was interrogated, questioned, poked and prodded and that was just what he could remember. He was used as a way to test the cure, and when he kept breaking the rules and finding answers about Meno, he assumed that they would kill him. Instead, they eventually simply left him to rot which, in this moment, he saw as a crueler fate.

Time passed quickly sometimes; most of the time it was unbearably slow. He was sleeping for most of it, begging that his dreams would have his loved ones in it, though he grew mad every time he woke up to being here.

He was drifting off into a beautiful dream where there was a clanging of hurried keys, a scream of his name from Penelope as she opened the door, and an unrecognizable woman nervously standing next to him. He shot up, kissing and hugging his wife, crying in her arms.

He shouted out desperately, "Please don't wake up! Please don't wake up!"

Penelope stepped back, looked into his exhausted eyes and said tearfully, "Honey, this isn't a dream. I'm actually here. I did it; we did it. You are free."

Tom refused to believe it. "This is the cruelest one yet," he said softly under his breath, too weak to hold himself up as he went to curl back into bed.

Penelope watched in horror. Her husband was reduced to bone and skin — no meat or muscle left. He had a long beard and even longer hair, and he was barely able to move. It killed her to see him like this. She felt responsible, as it had taken this long to get to him, but she was also very thankful that he was indeed still alive.

"I'm going to try and sleep this dream through; it's too much for me," he said, barely audible to himself.

Penelope put him over her shoulder in a fireman's carry and ushered for Jean to follow, entrusting in her the keycard.

"Do as I say and follow me," Penelope said, readjusting Tom, who even in his weakened state was proving to be wearing on her shoulder.

Penelope thought to herself that even though she was upset with Pat, in this moment she was thankful for his training.

'One can never be too strong,' his voice said in a thick, Irish accent in her head, with which she fully agreed.

"Ready?" Penelope asked.

Jean, in awe at this woman's will-power, thought to herself, *Who the hell are you?*

Her contemplation ended abruptly, though, as the building they happened to be in started to rumble, sprinklers went off and alarm bells triggered.

"Crap," Penelope said, as she hoisted Tom further on her shoulder.

"What did you do?" Jean asked, terrified.

Jean somehow found the next words out of Penelope's mouth to be less comforting than she thought they would be. "That was not me. We have to go now."

She then handed Jean the keycard and started running to the nearest emergency exit, which happened to be all the way down the hall.

"Open the cells; all of them!" Penelope shouted breathlessly, walking quickly to the emergency exit with Tom practically passed out on her shoulder.

Jean stood there for a moment, terrified to open the cells, worried about who or what was residing in them. But when she peered inside and saw nothing more than frail prisoners, she did exactly what Penelope asked and ran to open the exit door.

When they stepped out on the basement stairs leading to the main road, they saw hordes of people walking down the street with machine guns, shooting into the air, laughing and smiling to themselves in the most terrifying manner as they headed into the very building they were leaving.

Who the hell are these people? Are they from Kairos? Penelope thought to herself, trying to understand what was going on. All she could make out on one of the tattered leather jackets that one of the men wore was the faded letter 'H'.

Penelope ushered to Jean to keep quiet by pressing her finger to her mouth and staying below the exit, pressing herself against the cement walls that the stairs were hidden behind.

This was not part of the plan.

*

John was unsure what was about to happen. They had been working for so long to get to this point, to finally take down Menos and to finally save his father. His whole head was swimming with emotions: excitement, anxiety and anger.

It had been so long, and his father had been prisoner this whole time — the whole city had been prisoner this whole time. Decades of civilization numbed and used.

He hated that in this moment he also grew a horrid thought that was kismet.

He thought, for just a second, that he didn't want to remember; that he was in some way better not knowing. He held the empty vile in his hand with frustration, like he was somehow tricked into remembering all the terrible actions that led him here.

This, of course, wasn't true, and he felt sick for thinking it even momentarily, but the responsibility that grew was cripplingly. What if he didn't succeed? What if all those innocent people weren't able to be saved and this was their only shot? And most of all, was he actually qualified to try?

He heard his mother's voice in his head and used it as motivation.

'We have the ability and awareness to help —that's enough.'

But he couldn't help thinking, *Was it?*

The good memories came with it too, but in some way this made him even more anxious, for he remembered all that he risked losing, all that their society had at stake. Could they really fix this? Could Meno, after all these years, actually be stopped?

"John, hand me the map in the glove compartment," Ava said, tapping John on the shoulder.

He was abruptly brought back to awareness of being in the Bronco's passenger side, as Lily sped through a small unobscured opening in the nearest forest leaving Kairos. He took a second to register what she was saying then did as she asked.

"I know where I'm going, thank you," Lily said in rebuttal.

Ava rolled her eyes and grabbed the map from John with a soft 'thank you' in reply. "I know, dear, I'm just checking for an escape route."

Parker, who was sitting next to Ava in the back seat, tapped on her shoulder and signed, "Sure you are."

Ava smiled, winked and held up a finger to her mouth as if to say 'shh'.

They both chuckled, and Lily rolled her eyes having noticed them, as they weren't as sly as they thought they were.

John, however, did not notice any of this. He was still thoughtful, not paying much care to what was being conversed around him, fixating his attention on the empty vile in his hand that had once contained the antidote coursing through his system.

"Works like a treat, doesn't it?" Lily said, noticing what John was doing.

"Huh? Oh, yeah. Hubert seems to have succeeded, even with his limited supplies in Kairos," John said, shoving the bottle back into his pocket, still gripping it into his hand.

Lily chuckled at the fluidness of his knowledge that had been lacking just hours ago. She then nodded her head and thought to herself, *Hubert really does.*

"How is that old pain in the ass doing?"

Lily laughed. "Ah, surprisingly more of a pain in the ass. I'm sure having Mom back will help."

John nodded, thinking back to the friendship they had built over the years. Their mom was the only person he had really opened up to; these past years must have been hard. John then looked at his sister and it hit him; *This must have been horrible for her.*

"I'm sorry, sis, for all of this."

Lily looked over for a split second as she continued to speed through onto an abandoned highway. She shrugged as if brushing it off, but John could tell how much this whole situation bothered her.

"We had no choice. I'm just glad to finally have you back. Missed you."

John put a hand on her shoulder briefly. "I missed you, too. Well, you know what I mean," he said, poking fun at his predicament, knowing this would make Lily smile. It did.

"What did you do to your hair?" John joked, grabbing a bunch of her bright-red curls that used to be brown.

"It's called style, John."

John laughed. "Well, I like it. It's different, and I mean that as a compliment."

"The highest kind in my book," Lily said with a smile.

"How far are we from the city, anyway? It always feels like ages," Parker signed to Ava.

Ava replied, signing, "Don't worry, I'll wake you when we get there."

"Thanks," Parker replied. He leaned back in his seat and closed his eyes as if he really did intend on resting.

Ava shook her head at how relaxed Parker seemed to be, given the circumstances, and then went to read the map once more. Suddenly, something far off in the distance caught her attention instead. She nudged Parker in the arm roughly and ushered for him to follow her line of sight.

"Uh, guys. Is that part of the plan?"

They all looked up to see a massive cloud of smoke coming from the direction of the city. From the look on their faces, this was not part of the plan.

No one said anything.

Lily changed gears and sped up down the highway as fast as the Bronco would allow. "Why can't things ever be easy?" she said anxiously.

*

Forty Years Ago

A knock on the door cut the argumentative conversation inside its confinements to halt abruptly and rather annoyingly.

"Come in," a man answered.

The young man with a disheveled suit came hurriedly in, giving the impression that he had overslept and rushed out the door.

"Mr. Parley, so kind of you to join us an *hour* past the time we requested."

Mr. Parley started to apologize but the older man interjected, raising a hand to stop him.

"Just start the transcription, would you?" he said, with a roll of his eyes.

Instead of verbally responding, Mr. Parley simply pulled out his official notebook and pen in a hurried manner. The man who was a part of the discussion he was transcribing looked over in disgust as the young man stumbled with his pen and notepad.

He rolled his eyes before picking up where he was before the interruption. "As I was saying, there isn't a proper answer, Paul. Don't you understand that? Policy states we can't enact a climate accordance if it isn't put into an executive order, and our legislature hasn't been able to get enough of the people behind it. And even if we were able to miraculously get the vote, there isn't enough time. Don't you get that?"

"Yes but—"

"And let's not even mention the economic decline we are in, or social unrest, poverty rates rising... Tell me a way to fix any of these, and I'm on board; I'm with you."

The man he was supposed be having a conversation with, that seemed more of a yelling match, sighed in rebuttal. He, of course, didn't have these answers — no one did. If they did, then they wouldn't need to be having this conversation. So instead, he got frustrated, wondering why this was up to him to come up with such a difficult task. *Why does he get to be the one yelling and stating the obvious? Why does he get to be the one to give up?*

"So what are you saying, Jack? You want to stop trying? Just because we don't have an answer doesn't mean we never will."

"You go ahead and tell our citizens that. They want our heads!"

"Understandably they do, but it's our job to still keep presenting possible solutions, despite their pitch forks and knives."

Paul sat down in one of the large, brown chairs pinned with gold. He was exhausted, though they had only just begun.

Jack went over to his desk, for this was indeed his office, and pulled out a bottle full of light-brown liquid, and two crystal glasses. He filled them both with more than one would suggest for those discussing such important issues.

Paul sat up in a relieved manner as Jack came up and handed him one, sitting next to him in the other chair.

Jack took a sip as Paul just stared at his, running his fingers over the crystal rim.

"Why did you call this meeting if you are so against the topics we need to discuss?" Paul asked, in curiosity and fear. He had heard some speculations about Jack's current intentions but didn't want to give them too much grounding until he knew for sure.

Jack looked at him in a way that suggested he was unsure whether he should mention what they both knew he was getting to, so he took another large sip and spoke up. "I've recently been approached about a solution."

Paul, looking shocked, sat forward. "And here I thought this whole time that you were the most convinced we'd never find one. Well, don't leave me on the edge of my seat. What is it?"

"Oh, I still am. This solution is… unconventional."

Now Paul was concerned.

"What if we just take a break? Give the people a break?"

"And how exactly do you suggest we do that?" Paul said with a laugh.

"Have you ever heard of the philosophical puzzle, Meno? Plato coined it and gave it to his student, Aristotle."

"Yes, well in our position, philosophy is important to understand since we deal with ethics and sociological policies every day; so I am indeed familiar."

"So, you know the concept behind it."

"I mean, as best as one can. If one does not know x, they can't question x. If they know x, they still can't question x. No matter one's knowledge of x, or lack thereof, they can't debate it, and so on."

"Pretty much my understanding of it, as well. Obviously its highly debated, but it had me thinking. What if we could make our 'problems' x, or rather, what if the problem is us *knowing* what x is? Knowing the unsolvable problems we have created as a society. What if we were never meant to know what x is?"

Jack said this with a darkness behind his words that Paul mistook as naiveness, making him chuckle.

"It's that easy, like putting our problems in a metaphorical box on a shelf," Paul said jokingly, though he was the only one laughing.

"Well, kind of. More like allowing the people to. Removing x from the problem entirely...removing the inherent need to question. Just for a little while, so we can figure it out without the pressure."

"You can't be serious," Paul pressed, trying to make his fellow debater see reason, but he just sat there and took another sip from his crystal glass.

Paul looked away from him and looked out the window, where protesters still stood from early in the morning. *The anger on their faces... the fear.*

"It wouldn't be fair to use philosophies from Plato's and Aristotle on our modern problems," Paul pressed.

"I know that. I meant it more as an inspiration for giving this solution a chance."

"But it's not a solution. You see that, right?" Paul asked, concerned.

They'd been trying to find these answers for so long, and he feared that maybe his friend had finally snapped.

"I know. I've thought about these issues over and over again in my head, and I keep hitting the same walls. We both do, otherwise we wouldn't be here. So I stepped back and tried to look at it differently, thinking that maybe the question, or rather how we were asking it, was the problem. And I had a small thought that grew too big to ignore. That's why I'm here. To gauge your opinion on it. Maybe I'm crazy; I don't know."

Paul didn't say anything, for he was waiting on his next words to determine that.

"What if the problem is knowing? What if the problem is that our knowledge has grown so vast past our ability to fix what we have done? Like knowing when we are going to die —like our final punishment is to just accept our repercussions as a race."

"That's dark, even for you."

"I don't know about you, but I didn't expect that our mark on existence would come to the conclusion of being lighthearted."

Paul nodded. He got his point.

They both took another large sip of the beverages, fixating their attention on various objects around the room as if in deep thought about nothing in particular.

"Look, I'm not saying we stop trying, but at this point it doesn't seem possible... not soon enough to satisfy our current society. Why should they suffer like we must? At least until we find the answer, why must they know?"

"Oh? And what if we never find that answer or x?" Paul asked.

"Then they won't have suffered all those years worrying about something we couldn't fix anyway," Jack said, as if he believed this was a perfect plan.

"I don't know about this..."

"Just think about it."

Paul didn't say anything, and Jack didn't expect him to.

They just sat there sipping their drinks, giving off the impression that they had forgotten that Mr. Parley was there to transcribe everything with shaky hands...

It was quite and cold even with the fireplace roaring in the corner. So cold in fact that Mr. Parley felt his eyes fixate towards the fire in hopes of comforting him.

When suddenly something caught Mr. Parley's eyes. A letter on top of the scrap pile next to the fireplace to be used as kindling.

The envelope read:

Meno's pharmaceuticals, where our goal is your happiness.